# JACQUELINE NEW

# HAND
## OF THE
# WOLF

VINCI
BOOKS

Vinci Books

vinci-books.com

Published by Vinci Books Ltd in 2024

1

A CIP catalogue record for this book is available from the British Library.
Paperback ISBN: 9781036700065

Printed and bound in Great Britain by Clays Ltd, Elcograf S.p.A.

By Jacqueline New

Scars of the Past
Strains of Innocence
Hand of the Wolf

## Prologue

The hunter moved silently, each step careful and calculated, leaving barely a trace on the crisp earth beneath his feet. The air was filled with the scent of green needles and the earthy musk of damp soil. Here, the trees stood as ancient sentinels, their interlaced branches forming an impenetrable canopy overhead. They allowed no competition, reducing the sunlight that seeped through their woven branches to almost nothing. In this realm of shadows and muted light, the trees dictated the rules of survival, smothering the ambitions of any undergrowth daring enough to vie for a place under their dominion. At midday, the forest was dark. In places the ground brown, where the snow had failed to penetrate the forest ceiling. The hunter moved deliberately, keeping to the cover of the trees. He wore camouflage and a mask covering the lower part of his face. Dark intent eyes gazed through the shadowed ranks of trees. He barely blinked as he raised the rifle to his shoulder and looked into the sights mounted on top of the barrel. A hundred yards ahead, slightly below him, was a woman. Long, fair hair tied back and a pretty, round face. A beautiful face. For a moment, he lingered on her perfect features, magnified.

Gareth Bellamy smiled, following her with the sights as she moved. Annika Eklund was slim, blue-eyed and with pert breasts that she showed off with tight jumpers at every opportunity. Gareth had asked her out in the first week that he'd been at the Kingussie Wildlife Reserve, an expert in wolves and wildcats. Gareth was ex-army, a dog handler and marksman. He hadn't expected to find a job that might use both skills when he rejoined Civvie Street and went home to Inverness. Then the job had come up at Kingussie, tagging animals that lived on the reserve so they could be traced. And a month of training from a smoking hot Swede on the habits of the animals he was going to be tracking.

She'd been the one to shoot first. Gareth had crashed and burned with one word. Lesbian. Now he had her in his sights and she was oblivious to his scrutiny. It would take less than a second. She would know nothing about it. The sights dipped slightly, giving him a magnified view of her torso. The winter gear she wore covered up that body well. Gareth sighed and returned to his perusal of her face. A flash of white at the periphery of his vision came at the same time as Annika reached for a walkie-talkie.

"Alpha, one hundred yards ahead, passing a deadfall, heading uphill. Do you see her?"

Gareth's expert eyes darted to the flash of white, and he saw the wolf. Time for work. He was here because the vets at the Kingussie Reserve urgently needed to examine one of their charges. An animal that wouldn't come quietly. It was coming up the slope, facing him. Head raised, sniffing the air. Gareth had no doubt it knew where he was, Annika too,

2

though both wore a pungent scent to mask their own human smell. The vet, Colin McCauley, should be at the bottom of the hill and another sharpshooter fifty yards to Gareth's right, atop the ridge there. The wolf was passing into a circle formed by the four people. Gareth reached for the walkie-talkie fastened to the shoulder of his jacket and spoke softly.

"Gaz here. I have eyes. I see Annika and...I see you too, Taz. Colin, I can't see you, so keep your head down."

"Got you, Gaz. I don't have a clear shot," came Taz's reply.

"I've got the shot," Gareth said.

The entire exchange had taken place without the wolf leaving his sight. His finger applied gentle pressure to the trigger as the animal turned, presenting a side-on target. He adjusted his aim and slowly let out his breath, then held it.

He squeezed the trigger. The gun emitted a slight pop, and a second later, a bright flash of green appeared on the wolf's side as the dart found its mark. The animal bolted, moving from stillness to full sprint in a heartbeat. Within two strides, the fight-or-flight reaction had raised the animal's heartbeat, pumping the tranquiliser through its system even faster. It stumbled. Righted itself. Tried to run again. Fell.

"Alpha is down," Annika said. "Let's get her back to the Land Rover before the rest of the pack gets here."

———

"WE GOT to her just in time. Her stomach looks quite distended. There's some kind of infection there," Annika said.

She and Colin were back at the lab, the sedated she wolf on the table before them.

"I was thinking it might be torsion, but it's too high. Definitely upper GI, not lower," Colin replied, examining the gastrointestinal tract more closely.

They stood over the slumbering form of the Eurasian gray wolf. It looked like a dog, but with all the domesticity that humankind had bred into dogs stripped back. What was left was a majestic lean form strapped with muscle and a face that would stare down a man with ice-blue eyes. Even under the thick fur, the distension of the stomach was clear.

"There's something hard there," Colin said. "Could be an abscess has formed around whatever it is."

He was balding with glasses and a stomach that stretched the disposable plastic gown he wore. His brown eyes glanced at the monitor showing the wolf's vitals, picking out the key information from the dancing numbers.

"X-ray?" Annika suggested.

"Yes," Colin replied. "It's lucky our army boy didn't hit the stomach. The shock of that much pain might have killed her."

"He's an excellent shot," Annika said. "I don't think Taz could have got her from that distance. One thing he's got going for him, anyway."

"Any other positive traits?" Colin asked, looking over the top of his glasses.

Annika smiled. "Shall we focus on the job? I don't date where I work. I told you."

"Right. Just checking," Colin replied.

"I'm sure your husband would appreciate your interest in my love life," Annika said, crossing the clinic to a locked cupboard where the portable x-ray machine was located.

"I'm only looking out for you," Colin said, kicking off the locks on the wheels of the metal table where the wolf lay.

He pushed the table into the middle of the room, orientating it to make the animal's stomach accessible to the imaging machine.

"I've spent my career around dangerous predators. Gareth doesn't even come close," Annika said. "He's a child."

"He is, aye," Colin agreed. "A Ned, as we would say in Scotland."

"Ned?"

"Non. Educated. Delinquent. Probably straight into the Army at sixteen," Colin said. "Right. How's that looking?"

Annika switched on a monitor connected to the x-ray and made some adjustments. Colin arranged the screens over the parts of the wolf they wanted to protect. She wasn't just precious because she was a living creature. She was the alpha female of Kingussie's only wolf pack. And the pack was part of a global project to re-introduce the Eurasian Gray Wolf to Europe. The highlands of Scotland were one of the zones chosen for the program. On the basis that if it didn't work, the wolves would be confined to an island and more easily recaptured. Colin desperately hoped that wouldn't be necessary, though. The media and farmers as far away as Sussex were up in arms about the project. They were ignorant. Colin hated nothing more.

They completed the set-up of the x-ray with expert precision. Colin left the room while Annika took the pictures. Beyond the clinic was a corridor lined with maps of the Kingussie reserve and cross-section illustrations of wolf anatomy. A seating area at the far end of the corridor held Gaz and Taz, as they liked to be known. Two young men hired for their marksmanship more than their veterinary knowledge. Gaz raised a coffee cup in salute, his hair and beard auburn and his grin boyish. Taz was on his phone, his naturally anxious expression firmly in place, black eyebrows drawn down. Colin nodded to Gaz and stepped into the room next to the clinic, where a laptop would display the digitised results of the x-ray. Colin sat in a swivel chair and wheeled it across the lino floor to the laptop.

He heard someone coming along the corridor and didn't need to look up to know when Gaz stood in the doorway.

"How's the target?" he asked.

"Sleeping like a baby," Colin said. "Just waiting on the x-ray results coming up."

"Excuse me, Gareth," Annika said.

Gaz moved into the room, but not quite far enough that Annika didn't have to squeeze past him. Taz appeared behind and pulled Gaz fully out of the way by his sleeve. Gaz sniggered. Annika put a hand to the back of Colin's chair, the other on the desk, and ignored the marksman. Colin didn't know how she did it. He clicked into the x-ray translation software and they waited while it processed the images being transmitted digitally from the machine next door. They appeared on the screen in monochrome. Colin's eyes skipped to the area of the lump, but Annika saw it first.

"Vad Fan!" she exclaimed, resorting to her mother tongue for a moment. "What the hell is that?" she said, pointing.

Colin felt his stomach clench and the hairs on the back of his neck stand up. Gaz had come into the room and he swore, making him jump. Colin stared at the image on the

6

screen, at the foreign object in the wolf's stomach that had been causing her pain, bringing her to the attention of the veterinarian team he was part of. An object whose presence could mean the end of the project. He licked his lips, his mouth dry.

"We need to call the police," he said. "Now."

## Chapter 1

Mac watched the quayside through a steady drizzle. The windscreen wipers made a metronomic sound as they swiped. The rain pattered gently. Mac felt the tension within him that was the precursor to a full-blown panic attack. He took a breath, careful not to let on to his passenger. He repeated to himself the mantra he had devised during his sessions with his new psychiatrist. Not Doctor Siddhu, the police psychologist to whom visits were mandated after a traumatic incident. Mac didn't trust anyone contracted for Police Scotland. Didn't trust them not to get him suspended or pensioned off if he said the wrong thing.

Like, 'I almost beat a man to death once.' That was the memory that was always triggered by the rain. Sometimes it left him anxious and tense, liable to lash out at a subordinate. Other times, it crippled him. Now he told himself that the past was gone and could not be touched. Nor could it touch him. A memory was a collection of sense impressions. Sights. Sounds. Smells. All rendered impotent by the gulf of time. Skye was a long time ago. Mark Souter was a long time ago. Iona was a long time ago. Mac was present. The raindrops sluicing down the window of the car were present. The aftershave of Kai Stuart was present. The man who had just stepped out of the greasy spoon cafe at the end of the street was present.

"Guv," Kai said, superfluously.

"I see him. Let's go," Mac replied.

Kai stepped out of the car in lockstep with his guvnor. Both wore overcoats, long and dark. Both wore simple dark suits. For Mac, it was a simple choice to render the choice of wardrobe irrelevant. For Kai, it was probably in imitation of his boss. Ignoring the rain, Mac unbuttoned his overcoat and thrust his hands into his pockets. He started forward, Kai following a step behind and to the left. Ahead of them a tall, thin man with gaunt cheeks and sunken eyes was opening a golf umbrella. He held it over the door to the cafe, which opened for another man. He was average height with white hair and a seamed face. There was a smirk on that face, which was revealed, on closer inspection, to be a scar that pulled his mouth up at the left corner. The man wore a suit that hung on him loosely, as though he had lost weight recently through an illness. A scrawny neck with a large Adam's apple sat above a collar, buttoned and with a tie. He took a cigarette from an inside pocket of the overcoat he wore and the man beside him promptly produced a gold lighter and flicked it into life with one hand.

Mac ignored the puddles he splashed through as he strode forwards, not taking his eyes from the man in front of him. At the periphery of his vision, he saw movement, assumed there would be multiple bodyguards positioned around the designated meeting site. Another flicker of movement told him Kai was looking around, registering the circle of heavies into which the two policemen were walking. Mac smiled as he came to a halt a dozen feet away from the smoking man.

"Hance," he greeted casually.

"Smoke, Detective Chief Inspector?" Hance Allen offered the packet.

"Thanks," Mac acknowledged, stepping closer and taking one.

It was a cheap brand, as cheap as cigarettes got these days. The suit Hance Allen wore had signs of age and his shoes were the hard-wearing type old men bought for their permagrip soles in the icy winter. This was a wealthy gangster who still dressed as though he was a penniless nobody from Drumchapel. However long ago that was. The light was offered and Mac took a drag, his first in a long time. He'd had the same pack in a drawer of his desk for over a year.

"Do you smoke, Detective Sergeant Stuart?" Allen asked amiably, offering the pack to Kai.

"No," Kai said, shortly.

Mac watched Allen through a cloud of blue smoke coming from both of them. Allen looked back. He was showing off that he had sources of information inside the police, close to Mac's team. He knew Kai had been promoted a few months before.

"And how is DS Yun getting on with her new boss?" Allen asked.

"Laying it on a bit thick, aren't you, Hance?" Mac said, flicking the butt of the cigarette and sending a glowing ember to die on the wet cement.

"Am I? Just taking an interest in my friends, Mac. That's all. Nothing sinister."

"I get it. You've got coppers in your pocket. You know

how I take my coffee and what time I got into the office this morning. Let's move on."

"You asked for this meeting. Not me," Allen said, a touch of frost entering his voice.

"I did. And you accepted because you knew it was in your interests," Mac responded, just as hard.

"Alright, pal. You don't want to be friendly. Neither do I. Let's just get down to business, eh? Not for the first time."

Mac laughed. The last time he had spoken to Hance Allen was when one of his dealers had discovered the dead body of a customer. Allen had been on the phone with a solicitor to make sure his employee knew what to say and what not. And he hadn't been able to resist dropping little barbs that suggested Mac was in his pocket. Trying to undermine him in front of his team. That time, the witness had been Nari Yun. She'd requested a transfer to another DCI within twelve months. So, maybe the strategy worked. Mac had no concerns about Kai, though. As if reading his mind, Kai barked a laugh. Allen's eyes flicked to him for a moment.

"Something funny, pal?" he said, quietly.

"You. My guv isn't bent, so why don't you move on?" Kai replied with brazen insolence.

Mac suppressed a wince. Hance Allen was the kind to react viciously out of pure spite.

"We're here to talk to you about Sean Grant and Craig Kelly. They're John Lowe's boys, right?" Mac said.

"Wouldn't know."

"Employees," Kai said, making the question a statement.

"Why would I know who John Lowe employs?" Allen replied, finishing his cigarette and tossing it aside.

"They were known street dealers. Craig Kelly catering

to students in and around the Old Town. Grant was higher up the food chain, based in Craigmillar," Kai said matter-of-factly.

"I wouldn't know. I'm not a criminal," Allen told him. "Mac, going to keep your boy here muzzled before someone decides to smack him in the mouth?"

"Craigmillar is your territory," Mac said. "And Sean Grant was a trespasser. Two of your boys got the living hell kicked out of them two weeks ago in Craigmillar. And Sean Grant was moving onto their patch."

Allen sighed, squinting up at the sky.

"Can't remember the last time we had a decent bit of snow. I like cold weather. Like the snow. Can't stand this rain, though. All we seem to get these days."

"Hance. We have two murders of known dealers and before that a series of attacks on known associates of yours. This is starting to look like a war between you and John Lowe. My guv wanted me to reach out to you like this, off the record, to try and stop it escalating. I'm doing you a favour," Mac said earnestly.

Allen squinted at him, lips pursing before he spat. It hit the ground an inch from Mac's shoes.

"I run a haulage business, Mac. My dad built it up. I heard about Grant and Kelly. Heard they died hard. If I had a problem with someone, sabotaging my wagons for instance, I'd not do what was done to them. All that torture stuff. It's not the way a man does business."

Mac discarded his own cigarette and ran a hand through his hair, swiping it from his face.

"They died about as hard as it's possible to die. Like someone was sending a message to John Lowe," Mac said.

"I've got nothing to say to the guy," Allen replied.

"If you were unhappy with him sending his people onto your patch, you would want a message sent," Kai put in.

"Son, when you're a grownup, you can talk with the adults. Until then, haud yer wheesht," Allen snapped.

Mac suppressed a smile. Allen was holding onto his temper, and Kai was getting under his skin. If Allen hadn't been responsible for the murders of Craig Kelly and Sean Grant, he wouldn't be so sensitive about it. Wouldn't have even agreed to the meeting. This was him wanting the chance to feel out how much the police knew. And their chance to read him. He considered the idea of trying for an arrest. Would Allen's circle of bodyguards allow it? Stepping in to interfere in an arrest would be unequivocal criminal behaviour. And would prove that Allen had something to hide.

"That your lawyer?" Mac asked, pointing at the man holding the umbrella. "Looks different to the guy you sent to look after Chaz Pollock that time."

"This is my cousin. He's just visiting from Johnstone," Allen said.

"Really? I thought Davie Stokes was from Dalkeith originally," Mac said, glancing at the man, knowing exactly who he was and demonstrating to Allen that he knew his closest confederates.

"Moved to Edinburgh when he was fifteen. Did a stretch for possession and ABH three years ago. Won the lottery when he got out," Kai said, as though reading from a biography.

Davie Stokes held onto his boss's umbrella and didn't react.

"Or came into money somehow, anyway. Bought a house in North Berwick," Kai continued.

"Nice," Mac commented. "Neighbours with John-Boy? He's got three down that way."

Allen scowled at the mention of his son. Or possibly at the intimate knowledge the two coppers clearly had of his people and the way they hid their money.

"Nice party trick, boys. But this rain is terrible for my chest. If you're done, I need a slash," Allen said.

"No, we're not done. I've got two murder files on my desk and you're the prime suspect," Mac said harshly. "With the resources I've got at my disposal, I can crawl all over your business if I think you're involved. Finding out things that you'd rather were kept in the dark. I'm thinking this is just too blatant for you. You're risk averse in your old age, Hance. But, unfortunately for you, my guv likes you for both and sees this as an opportunity to clean house...."

"Are you finished?" Allen interrupted.

Mac took two steps forward until he towered over Allen. The sound of loud, heavy footsteps surrounded them suddenly. Davie Stokes had a hand in his jacket, eyes hard on Mac. But Kai had moved with his boss, turning slightly to put himself between Mac and Stokes.

"I wouldn't, pal," Kai said, and Mac knew he was grinning.

"I haven't even started, mate," Mac breathed in response to Allen's question. "I think this is some young crew wanting to impress you. I think you know who did these two and they've been quietly shipped out to Spain by now. I'm telling you that if you don't hand them over, then it won't just be Kenny Reid gunning for you. He'll have HMRC involved looking into how much tax you're paying and probably a list of unsolved cases he'd like to pin on you personally. And that's just for starters. So, make it easy on yourself, eh?"

Mac thought for a moment that he and Kai had pushed too far. There was death in the absolute stillness on Hance Allen's face. Davie Stokes wouldn't get the gun out of his coat before Kai dislocated his shoulder for him. But Mac knew there were at least four others, all packing. That was the risk with a gangster like Hance Allen. He worked hard to portray himself as an honest, working class man made good. But he could only be pushed so far before he snapped back. Mac stared him in the eye, unblinking. Rain ran down Mac's forehead and into his eyes, but still he refused to blink. The anxiety had his chest constricted so much he felt like he was in a vice. His stomach was clenched painfully.

"I'll say this once. And I'm doing you a favour because of what you did for my boy when your boss wanted to fit him up. I had nothing to do with those two. Nothing. If someone who knows me did it, thinking to impress me? Well, rest assured, Mac, they'll get what's coming to them for bringing you to my door. I'll be sure and give you a call when I've dealt with them for you."

Mac nodded once. Message delivered and Hance Allen shaken up. He hoped. If a body turned up, badly mangled and unidentifiable, there was a good chance Hance Allen had dealt with Mac's perpetrators. He didn't want that, but took some pleasure in causing Allen some discomfiture.

"Good talking with you, Hance," Mac said, turning on his heel.

A wall of men with faces like bricks stepped aside from where they had taken position behind him. Kai sauntered past, falling into step alongside his boss. He chuckled as they walked back to their vehicle. Mac found his shoulders tensing, waiting for a bullet in the back. He got into the car. Allen was gone, so were his bodyguards. As Mac turned the Audi his phone vibrated in his pocket. He held open his coat and Kai fished it out, answering the call and hitting the speaker.

"McNeill."

"Ben Musa here," said a deep voice, London accent.

"Yes," Mac replied, driving slowly back along the quayside.

The tarmac was black and shiny. Sky and sea were gray. Air was misty with the downpour. Mac wiped the rain from his face.

"Reid tells me you'd arranged an interview with Hance Allen," DCI Ben Musa said. "I was hoping you hadn't got to it yet."

"Just leaving. What's the problem?" Mac replied.

"Demarcation," Musa replied. "Craig Kelly and Sean Grant are Organised Crime's now. It's my case, and I didn't want your size twelves in it."

Mac gritted his teeth. "So, you're OC now," he said. "Last I heard you were Counter-Terrorism."

"Mayhew persuaded me. This case sits with my team now."

Mac resisted the urge to swear. Deputy Chief Constable Andrew Mayhew was not his biggest fan. He wondered if this was revenge. Mac had once undermined a case that Mayhew had taken public credit for closing. Compensation had been paid and heads had rolled. Not Mayhew's, of course. You didn't get to have the words Chief Constable in your job title without knowing how to insulate yourself from scandal. Or throw your subordinates under the nearest bus.

"Well, you're welcome to it," Mac said. "Speak to DI Barland…"

"Already have. I'm assigning one of my DCs to liaise with your team. Isla McVey. I know you've done a lot on this already. Want to make sure we don't miss anything."

"No bother," Mac said.

Case closed. DCI Benjamin Musa's Organised Crime Taskforce had the case now, a section within the Serious Crimes Unit but answerable to the Deputy Chief Constable rather than Detective Chief Superintendent Kenny Reid. Mac nodded to Kai, who hung up. The phone was ringing again before either of them could speak. Kenny Reid's name flashed up.

"I'm popular today," Mac muttered as Kai answered it.

"Mac," Reid's voice filled the car.

"Guv," Mac replied.

"I know you've just spoken to Musa. He made the call from my office. Think he's scared you would kick off."

Mac laughed. "Aye, right."

"You don't have the rest of the day off, if that's what you're thinking. I've got something for you. Pack a bag. You're going up to the highlands, son."

Mac glanced at the phone, then at Kai. "What the hell am I going up there for?"

"A call has reached me from a vet up at Kingussie, near Aviemore. An x-ray of a wolf has found a diamond ring in its stomach."

Reid waited for a beat. Mac didn't ask the obvious question, knowing there was more. Kai wasn't so controlled.

"A ring, sir? Isn't that more lost property?"

"Nae, lad," Reid replied, glee evident in his voice. "It's still attached to the finger."

# Chapter 2

**M**ac drove past the enormous sign proclaiming
Kingussie Wildlife Park, glancing over as he
did so. A pale, frigid sky framed it with a weak
sun shining above the dark hills beyond. He didn't know
much about this part of Scotland, but knew he was
following the A1 north. It was a black scar through a green
landscape, bringing back memories of Skye. It had been a
long time since a childhood spent outdoors. The road had
cleaved a narrow valley with precipitate hills rising to either
side, purple with heather, rising continuously. The landscape
had gone from being pretty somewhere around Perth to
brooding and ominous as he drove through the heart of the
highlands, picking up signs for Aviemore and Inverness.
The glens had been downright oppressive. Kingussie
wildlife park was situated in more open country, but those
damned black hills were all too close in the distance. Kai
was following somewhere behind, never more than two car
lengths away. Mac had the impression he'd have overtaken

another driver long ago but didn't dare be the boy racer to his guvnor.

Low-fi, distorted thrash metal almost drowned out the sound of the engine. Mac drummed his fingers on the wheel, letting the music vibrate into his soul, ripping anxiety apart like a thresher. In deference to his destination, he wore a fleece pullover with a polo-shirt collar visible beneath. Jeans and hiking boots.

A finger found in the stomach of a wild animal.

Christ, there would be so much countryside to endure with this one. He found himself gritting his teeth. Some tourist falls into the wolf enclosure and no-one notices until their finger turns up inside the belly of one of them. Somewhere there was a body and a verdict of accidental death. Or an entry for the Darwin Awards. It felt like a waste of time and he half thought he was on the case because Reid wanted to keep him out of Musa's way. Especially if Mayhew was backing Musa.

The head vet at the park, Colin McCauley, had told him to ignore the main entrance but head on for a mile to the service road. In another mile that would lead to the staff entrance and the veterinarian hospital. Mac forced his shoulders down, realizing they were rising with tension. The first eighteen years of his life had been spent roaming the wild country of Skye. He'd gone home to eat and sleep. Sometimes hadn't even done that. But after Iona and then his father's suicide, that had changed. He'd run as far and as fast as he could, ending up in Edinburgh, a world away from where he'd grown up. And the city had injected itself into his blood. Mac could walk a poorly lit underpass in Niddrie with more confidence than a woodland trail. Not for the first time, he issued a few choice swearwords in his head to Kenny Reid. Seeing the turning up ahead, he turned, noting Kai indicating behind him. Melissa was back at HQ with DC McVey, ensuring a smooth handover of the two murder cases to the OCT. Kai wasn't too bad these days. A useful right hand in certain situations, if still lacking his DI's intuition. But he made up for it with dogged perseverance and an engaging personality. A good contrast to Mac's proclivity for glowering.

The trees drew close. The road narrowed, widening frequently to allow passing places before shrinking again. Greenery joined overhead, turning the road into a tunnel, filtering the wan sunlight. Glancing to the side revealed only the shadowed depths in between thick undergrowth. He felt a fleeting sensation of claustrophobia and brought his mind back to the Norwegian band playing from his phone to the car's speakers. A crushing, saw-toothed guitar took on an interesting riff, and it made Mac feel armed against the smothering, encroaching nature. It was ridiculous. Anyone else would rave about the beautiful scenery, but he'd take tower blocks and industrial estates any day. Finally, a gate appeared. Beyond it was a series of buildings, clearly pre-fabricated. All were single-story and flat-topped, doors reached by ramps and connected to each other by plastic fronted corridors. A small car park was situated just inside the gate. A collection of modest hatchbacks with mud-splattered wheel arches and boots alongside liveried Land Rovers in an even worse state.

A man in green wellies, cords, and a wool jumper with patches on the elbows was vaping by the gate, pacing a few steps back and forth as he did so. As Mac pulled up, he hurried to the wire-mesh gate and waited as Mac got out. The silence hit Mac like a hammer. He didn't like it. Approaching the man, he took his warrant card from the pocket of his jeans.

21

"DCI McNeill, Police Scotland. That's my sergeant, DS Stuart, just coming up the road. We're looking for Doctor Colin McCauley?"

"That's me," Colin said, stuffing the vape into his pocket.

He was round in the stomach and face with thinning hair. He took a key from a lanyard worn under his jumper and opened a padlock, pulling back a bolt and opening the gate. After Mac had driven in and parked, he offered an outstretched hand. The handshake comprised a brief grasp of Mac's fingers and a forced smile. This was a man unused to dealing with police and shaken up by the experience. Kai pulled in moments later. Mac greeted him with a nod as Colin relocked the gate, then led them towards one of the buildings. On the other side of the car park, he saw two men smoking cigarettes and watching him and Kai. One had auburn hair and a beard, the other was Indian or Pakistani at a glance.

"Thank you for responding so quickly, Inspector. Is that the correct title?" Colin said, opening the door for them.

Mac entered ahead of him, finding himself in a reception area. A corridor led on from a curving desk on which three phones sat and a couple of laptops. The walls were papered with flow-charts and illustrative cross-sections of animal physiognomy. Dogs seemed prevalent. There was a stack of wire cages beside the door and an opened box containing some kind of medical supplies. It felt more like a field hospital than a clinical setting.

"Apologies for the mess. We've been moved into this section while the main building is renovated. We got an EU grant just in time. Brexit, you know," Colin said. "It'll be great when it's finished. State-of-the art. Until then, I'm afraid we're in the Portakabins," he laughed nervously.

"Better than my flat, Doctor McCauley," Kai said with an amiable smile.

"Do you want to see the er...object?" Colin asked.

Mac thrust his hands into his jeans, dark eyes flicking around the room before resting on Colin.

"Lead on," he said.

Colin guided them behind the reception desk and through double doors, then along a narrow corridor with doors leading off to both sides. Through one that was open, Mac saw what looked like a treatment room. Another was marked as a supply cupboard. At the end, the corridor turned ninety degrees. They went through another door and round another corner, contributing to a feeling of disorientation. Finally, Colin pushed open a door marked Lab 1, printed on a piece of laminated A4 paper, and tacked up. Inside was a room with two windows, looking out over the trackless forest. A surgical table stood to one side and a lab bench opposite, complete with three metal stools. A cabinet of dark glass bottles and white boxes of pharmaceuticals covered an entire wall next to the door. Three wide fridges were stacked one atop the other next to it, clipboards attached to their chrome metal doors with pens attached to each by string.

"We extracted the...thing surgically. The ring posed too much of a risk to Friga's health to let it work its way through her lower GI system. And we thought her digestive juices would make identification more difficult."

"I think you probably thought right, Doctor," Mac said. "Bare bones wouldn't give us much to go on."

"We put it in the sample fridge. We weren't sure how long it would take the police to get here."

He walked to the fridges, opening the middle one and took out a plastic box. Mac caught the sound of shifting ice within. Colin put it down on the bench and stepped back, leaning on the surgical table, hands behind him.

"You have some surgical gloves?" Mac asked.

Colin had been staring at the box and jumped at the question. He hurried to a cupboard and produced a cardboard box of gloves. Mac and Kai took a pair each. Then Mac opened the box. Nestled on the ice was a slender finger. In size and shape, it looked female. It wore a ring with a large stone at its centre and several smaller gleaming stars around the band.

"Diamond?" Kai asked.

"I'm not a jeweler, but it looks like it to me," Mac replied.

The tip of the finger was gone, bone protruding from the mangled, stiff flesh. There was a bluish discolouration just visible where the bone emerged. Mac peered closer.

"Is that a tattoo?" he said aloud.

"Could be. Hard to say," Kai replied, also bending close.

"This wasn't cut neatly. I've seen fingers removed with bolt cutters, pliers, knives…this was chewed, I think. Would you agree, Doctor McCauley?" Mac asked, looking back over his shoulder.

Colin was looking distinctly gray. He gave a hasty nod and started to speak, then seemed to think better of opening his mouth.

"I'm sorry…I…"

The door to the room opened and a Valkyrie stepped in. That was the word that leaped straight into Mac's head. Scandinavian. Viking. She was tall, only a little shorter than Mac. White-gold hair was tied back in a severe ponytail, scraping her hair right back. Blue eyes. High cheeks. Athletic figure. Strong, but without losing femininity. Mac straightened from the dismembered finger, waiting for the newcomer to be introduced. Kai cleared his throat and shifted his posture, standing with feet apart and hands clasped in front of him. The boy couldn't help himself.

"I'm Doctor Annika Eklund," she said in a strong Scandinavian accent. "I'm the Director of the Kingussie Rewilding Project. You must be the policemen."

"Detective Chief Inspector McNeill," Mac said. "This is Detective Sergeant Stuart."

Kai nodded, and Annika's eyes flicked between them. Mac had the sense of being weighed and measured. He was sitting back against the bench, almost slouching, arms folded. He hadn't touched the finger yet but kept his gloved hands out of contact with anything but air, regardless.

"Colin, are you OK?" Annika said, noticing his sickly expression.

She put a hand to his back, rubbing gently. Mac wondered immediately if they were a couple.

"Sorry, um, having some trouble with…human…body parts. Excuse me."

Colin practically ran from the room. Kai gave a soft snort of laughter. Annika turned to them.

"Colin is an excellent surgeon but can't stand the sight of blood when it's related to people."

"Understandable. This is a pretty gruesome find," Mac said, turning back to the grisly item in question. "I thought he would be in charge. I was told he was the head vet here."

"He heads up our veterinary and surgical team and works for the park. I'm in charge of the project involving the wolves," Annika replied.

"Project?" Mac asked.

"We are trying to reintroduce native animal species back into their legacy habitats. Wolves were once native to all

25

areas of northern and western Europe, but they've been driven out by human activity."

Mac nodded, digesting that. It didn't matter to him who he was dealing with, as long as he knew who they were. Regardless of hierarchy, he was enjoying dealing with Annika over Colin. "Obvious question, but I take it you haven't had any tourists go missing or falling into the wolf enclosure? It was a wolf, wasn't it?"

"Yes, it was. Friga, the alpha female of a five animal pack. And our wolves are not part of the safari park. They roam free in an area not open to the public," Annika replied, joining them at the bench and looking down at the finger with clinical dispassion.

"Roaming free?" Kai said, sounding surprised.

"Not completely. The wolf pack was brought over from Serbia, where a larger pack is being reintroduced. The fact Britain is an island made it ideal for the project. The Kingussie Park received money from the EU and a substantial legacy of land from the Laird of Strathspey in his will."

"You said not completely roaming free," Mac said. "So the animals are still enclosed?"

"For now. They have a private enclosure around five hundred square kilometers."

"Can the enclosure be easily accessed?" Mac asked.

Annika pursed her lips for a moment, folding her arms. Blue eyes as sharp as shattered ice held Mac's gaze. "You can't guarantee security over that kind of area, especially with a highland landscape. The fences are high and there is plenty of signage warning of private property and prosecution for trespassers."

Mac sensed she was choosing her words carefully and with good reason. If it turned out a wolf had escaped or someone strayed inside the enclosure, it would probably spell trouble for Annika's project. That kind of thing made the media salivate and politicians jumpy.

"Is there any surveillance?" Kai asked. He had his phone in hand and was typing out notes.

"In areas the wolves frequent, yes. We've set up static cameras where we're most likely to observe them. And there are some cameras at strategic points around the fencing. But, our funds were mostly used up enclosing such a large area adequately. We had little left over for hi-tech security," Annika replied.

"I don't think this finger was removed before the wolf got to the hand. It looks like it's been gnawed rather than cut. So, I'm thinking that we're looking for someone who was either dead in the enclosure and found by your wolves. Or was killed by them," Mac said.

"They are timid of humans. They wouldn't hunt us," Annika said, voice dropping in temperature.

Mac held up his hands. "I'm not here to hurt your project, doctor. I just want to find out who this belonged to and how she died. Assuming she is dead."

"Where's the rest of her if she was dead and thrown to the wolves?" Kai asked.

"Devoured," Annika replied simply. "It would only take two or three days for a pack to consume a body. What they couldn't eat would have been buried. It's a large area, as I said before. I doubt any remains will be found."

Kai glanced at Mac, an eyebrow raised. Mac nodded. So they had a victim but no official crime scene. Well, he relished a challenge, and it had been a bit quiet lately.

# Chapter 3

"Is she serious? She wants to have wolves wandering about the place?" Kai said in a half-whisper.

He and Mac stood over a coffee pot in the corner of a staff room, further into the complex of connected temporary buildings from the lab. An assortment of mismatched furniture shared the space with pot plants and veterinarian periodicals on a coffee table. Mac spotted a copy of FHM poking out from under one of the scientific journals. Windows on one side of the building looked out on the woods that crowded close. The ground under the trees was desolate, brown with dropped needles and dirt, dark with the shade of the interlocking canopy above. A dark, forbidding forest. Like something out of a fairy tale. And with bloodthirsty monsters haunting the shadows? It was silly, but there was a possibility that someone had been stalked and killed by the inhabitants of that wood. Beyond the fencing he couldn't see but assumed was there. Call it a copper's skepticism, but Mac just couldn't take Annika's confident assertion at face value.

"Aye, she's serious. Sounds mad, I know," Mac said.

A train of thought was unfolding in his mind. This kind of project was always prey to protests. Animal rights, farmers, the not in my backyard brigade. Could one of them have broken into the enclosure intending to stage something or even releasing the wolves? Ended up becoming prey? It was a possibility. Or just an idiot, climbing a fence to get a look. Or, god forbid, a selfie with the wolves. Plenty of people died in stupid ways every year.

"It's crazy! So, a family goes up into the Pentlands for a picnic and ends up getting munched themselves. And what's stopping them from coming into the towns?"

Kai shook his head, blowing on the black coffee he'd just poured for himself into a mug from a supply stacked beside the machine.

"Not our place to speculate. They're here and someone has lost at least a finger to them," Mac said. "Our job is to find out who and establish if a crime has been committed."

He sipped his own coffee. It tasted like burned wood. Annika had taken them to the staff room while she dug out maps of the area. Paper maps. Mac was happy enough with sat nav, but it wouldn't be much use out in the woods. They needed something that showed all the little paths and trails that the park rangers had made or discovered. A pathologist had been assigned from a station up in Inverness; it was closer than Derek Stringer, who served as police pathologist in Edinburgh. Mac doubted Stringer would lower himself to put on wellies and tramp about the woods. He'd been known to turn up at a crime scene in black tie, having been taken away from the opera or some such high-brow entertainment. Doctor Hayley Blackwood was on her way, though Mac didn't yet have a scene of death for her to look at. She would examine the finger if only to give official confirmation of what Mac already knew. It had been bitten or gnawed from the hand and bore part of a tattoo. A door leading into the staff room opened and Mac looked up, expecting Annika Eklund.

Instead, one of the two men he had seen outside smoking stepped in. His reaction to seeing Mac and Kai was to freeze, eyes widening slightly before a wide-boy grin covered the surprise. Mac had seen the reaction on about a thousand faces over the years, usually from people who were afraid of the police. In his experience, that meant people with something to hide. He turned to face the newcomer, putting his mug down.

"Hi," the man said.

He had auburn hair and a beard. After a beat, he put out his hand. Mac took it, clasping it firmly and holding the other man's gaze.

"You must be the policemen from Edinburgh," he said.

English accent. Newcastle, though Mac couldn't really tell Tyneside from Durham or Northumberland.

"DCI McNeill," he said. "This is DS Stuart."

Kai nodded.

"Gaz," the man said.

"Gaz?" Kai asked.

"Um...Gaz Bellamy. Gareth Bellamy. I work here," he said.

Kai nodded.

"So, what brings you all the way up here?" Gaz said, still standing in the doorway somewhat awkwardly.

There was a moment of silence. Mac glanced at Kai. "You didn't know?" Mac asked.

Gaz shrugged. "Annika hasn't said anything." He licked his lips and his hand went to the pocket of the army surplus jacket he was wearing.

Mac's eyes went to that pocket as well. Gaz noticed and removed his hand, stepping back from the doorway into the corridor and renewing the grin. This was a man hiding something, without question. Something that would fit into a pocket. Mac's guess would be a bag of weed. Maybe some pills. The kind of thing that makes you jumpy when you open a door and find two policemen on the other side.

"Doctor Eklund believes criminal behaviour might have occurred up here, and we got the call," Mac said.

He folded his arms and turned himself to face the door fully. The movement prompted Gaz to back away a couple more feet. From Gaz's position, the wall blocked his view of Kai. Mac was aware of Kai moving quietly towards the other door that also led into the staff room. It opened out onto the same corridor in which Gaz was standing, just around a corner. Mac heard the stealthy click of the door opening. Kai was reading the situation with the instinct of a predator scenting blood, positioning himself to cut off a retreat. Mac couldn't remember where the corridor went in the opposite direction but thought it came to a dead end, a window looking out over the car park. It had only been the briefest of glimpses as Annika had ushered him into the staff room.

"Something wrong…Gaz?" Mac asked, quietly.

That was when Gaz bolted. Mac lunged to the door, grabbing the frame to swing himself through. Gaz had run straight into Kai, who dropped his shoulder and rugby tackled him to the ground. Gaz went down kicking and shouting. Mac heard running footsteps from further down the corridor and a man of Indian or Pakistani ethnicity appeared through a door. He was wider than Gaz and taller. Black curly hair and a beard that didn't cover his upper lip. He ran down the corridor and seized Kai by the back of his collar, hauling him bodily from Gaz and throwing him against the wall.

"Get off him!" he snarled at Kai. "You OK Gaz? Gaz?"

Gaz had scrambled to his hands and knees. Mac reached him, grabbed for one foot, but he had the desperation of a cornered rat and kicked out with more force than Mac was ready for. A boot caught Mac low and sent him reeling and gasping. Then Gaz was on his feet and running hard. His rescuer stared after him, openmouthed. Kai wrenched himself free, seized the man by the front of his t-shirt and slammed him into the far wall.

"You're under arrest for assaulting a police officer," Kai grated, grinning with bared teeth and a face red with anger.

He spat the man's rights at him as Mac picked himself up, wheezing. The man he held had eyes like plates now, white all the way around. His mouth opened and closed like a stranded fish.

"You're coppers!" he finally managed.

"Aye," Mac said, straightening. "And you're about this close to falling down stairs while resisting arrest."

He was angry. Feeling somewhat humiliated and embarrassed. He was up in the backside of civilisation, investigating what would, in all likelihood, be ruled death by misadventure. Meanwhile, the case of his career was in the hands of superhero cop and media darling Benjamin Musa. There was a rumor that the Idris Elba character Luther was loosely based on Musa. A chance to take down Hance Allen. Mac wanted it. But here he was. Looking into the contents of a wolf's stomach. He wanted to hit someone.

"What?" the man stammered, eyes swiveling from one hard-faced, angry cop to another.

He gulped and raised his hands as though in surrender.

"Want to tell me why you just put yourself neck deep in

the brown stuff?" Kai said, shoving his face just inches from the other mans.

"You were attacking my mate. I didn't know you were cops."

Mac heard Midlands in his accent. Another Englishman.

"Who are you, pal?" Mac asked, still slightly breathless, although the white-hot knife stabbing pain in his groin had subsided.

"Taz. Taz Khan. I'm a ranger," Taz replied. "So's Gaz. We were both hired at the same time because we're good shots."

"Good shots?" Kai demanded.

"They needed expert marksmen so they could tranquil-lise the animals to tag them or bring them in for examina-tions and surgery. I'm ex-job. Armed response. Come on lads, give me a break, yeah?"

Kai glanced at Mac, who could see the sudden empathy in his sergeant's face. Kai had an automatic loyalty to other officers and that extended to ex-coppers. Mac didn't care what Taz used to be. He cared about why Gaz tried to run and whether Taz was involved in the reason for his legging it.

"From this angle, it looks like your mate had something to hide and you helped him get away. Aiding and abetting. Accessory to…what?" Mac asked.

Kai released his hold on Taz, stepping back a couple of feet.

"Nothing. I score a bit of weed off him. I don't know about anything else he's into. Don't even know him that well. We just clicked over guns, yeah? And we both got knocked back by the ice queen."

"What is the meaning of this!" Annika Eklund stepped through the same door that Taz had appeared through.

She carried rolled papers under her arm and was looking at the tableau with wide eyes. But while Taz's white-rimmed stare was pure terror, Annika just looked like a Viking about to split some heads. Kai stepped away from Taz further, suddenly looking guilty. He may have impressed Mac enough recently for Mac to support his promotion, but his thinking still originated south of his beltline sometimes. Mac planted a heavy hand on Taz's shoulder, letting him know that running wasn't an option.

"I just saw Gareth Bellamy running for his life, and you have another of my staff up against a wall?" Annika said, stalking along the corridor.

She shoved the rolled papers towards Kai, who found himself taking them before he realised what he was doing. Mac caught Taz saying something under his breath in another language. Urdu perhaps. The look he gave Annika from below his brows was more resentment than fear.

"Gareth Bellamy tried to run from us for no conceivable reason. We pursued, and this man intervened, assaulted DS Stuart," Mac told her, matching her tone for steel.

Annika looked at Taz, who glanced at her, eyes skittering from her stabbing blue-eyed stare. Her blonde brows were drawn down, mouth tight.

"I was just telling them. I don't know why Gaz ran. I didn't know they were police," he muttered.

"He had something in his pocket that he didn't want us to see," Mac said. "I'm thinking recreational drugs. He also didn't know why we were here. If he had drugs on him, he probably assumed we knew and were here for him."

"That's a lot of presumption, Detective Chief Inspector," Annika said frostily.

"He ran and fought hard to get away. That's a fact," Mac shot back.

They stood facing each other, Taz in between looking from one to the other in bewilderment.

"Gaz has rooms on site. I will search them myself…"

"You won't. My sergeant will search them," Mac interrupted.

"You can't possibly suspect that I would…"

"I don't suspect anything, but I want to know what he wants to hide so badly he's willing to lose his job," Mac again cut across her.

His anger was under control, but her eyes had lit brighter when he'd interrupted her. There were spots of colour in her cheeks and Mac found the sight of anger in her attractive. He cut across her to see that flash of anger again.

"OK. I'm not happy about this, but I want this sorted out and to get back to my work," Annika finally said, pursing her lips. "Taz, show the sergeant where Gaz's rooms are."

"Any idea where Bellamy might have gone?" Mac asked.

"He was running towards the car park. His vehicle was there, so…anywhere by now," Annika said.

Mac breathed out sharply through his nose. It probably had nothing to do with his case and only involved the most trivial of criminal behaviour. But it galled him that Gaz had got away. A policeman's instinct. Plus, he was seriously pissed at the kick to his nuts.

"He'll keep. Kai, see what you can find in his room. And you…" he pointed at Taz, about to deliver a threat to ensure good behaviour. He looked at Annika and thought better of it. "Behave yourself," he finished lamely.

Kai took Taz by the elbow. The other man pointed

JACQUELINE NEW

down the corridor, and Kai allowed him to go first, following him closely.

"I'm sorry for the commotion, Doctor Eklund," Mac said, knowing he needed to rebuild some bridges. "If we could have a look at those maps?"

Annika looked after Taz and Kai, frowning before giving a curt nod.

"I'm sorry too, Detective Chief Inspector. In truth, Gareth has been a problem since he arrived. I only kept him on because he's a superb marksman. Ex-military and never misses. But he's been a pest to some of the female staff, including me. You'd be amazed how many of the women working here turned out to be lesbians after he arrived," she said with a small smile.

She was offering an olive branch, and Mac returned the smile. He opened the door to the staff room and stepped aside for Annika to precede him.

"Detective Chief Inspector is a mouthful. You can call me Mac. Everyone does," he said.

"I will call you Detective Chief Inspector," Annika said as she passed him.

# Chapter 4

Mac suppressed a smile as he followed Annika back into the staff room. She quickly and efficiently cleared the coffee table of magazines, only pausing at the FHM. She grimaced over the image of the woman on the cover.

"Gareth Bellamy is a juvenile," she said with disgust.

She rolled the magazine up and deposited it in a pedal bin beside the table on which the coffee pot sat. Shaking her head, she picked up two books to weigh down the rolled map that Mac had spread out.

"Now. This is a map of the wolf enclosure. We are just off the map down here. This is the observed range that the wolves occupy based on our tracking data."

She took a highlighter from her pocket and began marking out a large area. It took up the lion's share of the enclosure. Mac was leaning over the map looking for roads or trails that led into the enclosed area. He pointed to one which snaked around the outside of the enclosure to the west, appearing from the bottom of the map. It ended halfway up where it was joined by another, which came in from the left-hand edge. A building was marked where the two roads met.

"What are these roads?" he asked.

"The one coming up from the south is an old trail that used to run down to the main road into Kingussie. It served the crofts in this area of which there are none any more. We use it, but it's only really passable with a good four by four or a quad. There are several streams crossing it that flood in bad rain. We get a lot of bad rain."

"And this building?"

"An old church. Derelict now. Hasn't been used for a very long time," Annika said.

"What about the road coming in from the west, ending at the church? Where does that go?"

"That was used by our contractors to get materials to the west side of the enclosure when the fences were being put up. It's gated at the church and I don't think anyone else uses it."

"What's over there?" Mac asked, pointing to the area off the right side of the map beside the church.

"Nothing. Just hills. Keep going that way and you'll eventually reach Loch Gynack."

Mac nodded, lost in thought. There were two possibilities. Either someone had been killed and brought to the enclosure to be disposed of. Or they had brought themselves there and been disposed of by the wolves themselves. Either way, they had got into the enclosure somehow. The question was where?

"If someone got in, how quickly would the wolves know about it? I mean, smelling them or hearing them or something?"

"Like I said, Detective Chief Inspector," Annika said

with a direct stare. "They are shy of humans. These are not sharks. They may well have caught the scent of someone blundering about in the woods. It would just have made them move away. These animals are not to blame."

Mac raised a hand in surrender. He needed Annika's cooperation. She was clearly extremely protective and knowledgeable about her project and the park in which it was situated. The rangers should also be knowledgeable, but so far he wasn't convinced about Taz and Gaz. Was suspicious, in fact.

"What about if a body was left inside? How long then?"

"Obviously, it would depend on how far away they were when it was left."

Mac grimaced. Fair point.

"We need to find out where this person got inside. Or where they were taken inside. Is it possible to drive around the perimeter of the enclosure, so we can examine the fences?"

Annika pursed her lips, looking down at the map intently. "No, there are sections where the only way to get around is on foot and the area is very large. We have CCTV coverage at various points. We can check the footage there. Where there aren't cameras, there are some places that we could drive to."

"How many does that leave where there's no coverage and no accessibility by car?" Mac asked.

"About twenty-five percent. Perhaps a little more," Annika said after a moment's thought. "Mainly this area where the enclosure climbs the slopes of Creag Righ Tharailt, a mountain to the west of the park," she traced a line on one part of the map in which close packed lines indicated a steep slope. "And around here, near a woodland copse."

It wasn't great. That twenty-five percent could be hiding a crime scene.

"On the cameras you have, how many people could you lend to me to check footage, say, for the last twenty-four hours?" Mac asked.

"Me and Graeme," Annika said. "That's Graeme McKay, he's my graduate assistant, and he maintains our tech. The static cameras we have are motion triggered. We can check to see if any of the footage we have indicated this person. Or the wolves eating her."

She showed no sign that she had issued such a grisly statement, behaving perfectly matter-of-factly. Mac found himself wondering what would faze her. He watched her intently, not realizing he was staring until she lifted her eyes from the map. Mac quickly looked down before their eyes met. In the corner of his eye, he was aware of her gaze fixed on him for a long moment. Then her head moved, and she was looking back at the map. They stood almost shoulder to shoulder, their bowed heads only inches apart. Mac told himself this wasn't the time to be admiring a woman. He tried to shut the thoughts of just how attractive she was from his mind. A scent reached him. Not perfume. Clean and fresh, deodorant and soap. Subtle and feminine.

"Then we have the beginnings of a plan," Mac said. "How populated is this area?"

"Not very. Highland population density is generally low. Kingussie is the nearest town with Aviemore the next closest and much bigger because of the tourist trade."

"Lots of holiday lets around here, I bet," Mac said.

"Lots. There isn't much of a year round population. That's why the park was built here and why I chose the site for the project."

"Do you have a map that shows any of these lets?" Mac asked.

"No," Annika shook her head. "I have topographical, geological, but nothing like that. I couldn't even tell you from my own exploration. We don't exactly have housing estates up here, you know? Any houses are generally tucked away for privacy."

An idea occurred to Mac, and he grinned. He remembered a conversation with Clio, one of the few people he counted as a friend. Possibly the only one. They had talked of getting away with Clio's daughter, Maia. An Airbnb somewhere. Mac tended to be forced to take holidays, receiving irritated emails from his unit's HR liaison. Generally, time off for him meant counting the days until he was back at work. But meeting Clio had begun to change that. A different side to him came out when he was with her and Maia. Now, he opened the app and initiated a search for properties in his current area. Soon icons appeared, overlaid on the map of this part of Scotland. There weren't many. He wondered what other companies offered a similar service. Kai might know. There were always estate agents. Zooming in on the map, he saw a house not far from the wildlife park. Not listed as a holiday let, just visible on the map.

"You know where this place is?" he asked.

Annika looked and shrugged. "Haven't seen it or met anyone who lives there."

Mac looked at the satellite view of the map but couldn't make out a road leading to the house from the main A road, which ran more or less north to south from Perth to Inverness. There must be one, but it was perhaps no more than a track. It was somewhere to start, anyway. The phone chimed and Kai's name appeared. Mac swiped up and turned away from Annika.

"Guv, found something in Bellamy's room. Didn't want to leave it with this guy hanging around."

Mac assumed he meant Taz and understood Kai calling him instead of reporting in person. If he believed the room contained evidence, he would want to secure it.

"I'll be right there," Mac said, hanging up.

Annika was looking at him, one golden eyebrow raised, arms folded. Questioning.

"Could you point me toward Gareth Bellamy's room?" Mac asked.

"Sure, I'll take you. What's wrong? Did your sergeant find something?" Annika asked, leading the way out of the room.

"Yes," Mac said abruptly, wanting to discourage further questions.

She looked over her shoulder at him. Mac's mind was leaping ahead. Gaz Bellamy had something to hide and Kai had found something serious. A woman was dead and apparently Bellamy was a pest to women around him. Did that mean a predator? Or just a typical lad who fancied his chances with any female who walked across his path? Annika led him out of a door and down a ramp that ran along the side of the building. They crossed a small gravel space in which a shed stood, fenced and gated. A sign on the fence announced danger due to high voltage. Cables ran along the ground and into the nearest building. Beyond was an area of grass and more pre-fabricated buildings. Another ramp and she led him into a corridor lined with doors. Names were printed on A5 pieces of laminated paper, taped to the plywood doors. A noticeboard hung on a wall opposite one door, a window looking

42

out onto bins opposite another. Taz stood outside a room, fidgeting. Kai stood opposite, his back to the entrance, face blank in a way that only a copper on sentry duty could manage. Impassive, unresponsive, and useless to try and talk to.

On seeing Mac, he opened the door with his hand covered by the sleeve of his jacket. They had both previously discarded the surgical gloves they'd worn to examine the finger. Mac thrust hands into the pockets of his jeans. Kai stepped into the room and Mac followed, closing the door on Annika as she was opening her mouth. He looked at Kai and raised an eyebrow. The room was a modestly appointed bedroom of the student accommodation style. A single bed stood against one wall. A cheap computer desk at the foot of the bed with a wheeled swivel chair in front of it. The chair had a hole in its upholstery, revealing foam beneath. A washbasin occupied the wall opposite the desk, a bookcase, and armchair next to it. The chair was the kind you found in hospital waiting rooms. It looked uncomfortable. The room was decorated in cream and beige except for several luridly colored pinups, all of naked or semi-naked women. There was a strong smell of stale smoke, with an underlying bitterness that Mac recognized as weed.

Kai stooped next to the bed and fished a pen from his pocket. He reached under the bed and brought out a plastic bag, pen hooked through the handles. Mac expected to see a stash of marijuana. He squatted next to Kai as he opened out the bag. For a moment Mac frowned into the depths, not understanding exactly what he was seeing. It looked like a bundle of fabric. Then he saw it. Kai reached in and hooked a pair of women's underwear from the collection in the bag. It was blue, edged in lace, but not exactly sexy. More like an everyday pair. There was a dark stain on one side, just below the waistband. Against the blue, it looked black.

"Blood?" Kai said.

"Looks like it to me. How many are in there?"

"I'd say about five or six. Nothing too sexy. Pretty ordinary. Maybe our boy is a cross dresser," Kai said. "Or a pantie sniffer."

"Doesn't seem the type to be wearing them. Annika says he's a pest."

"Annika?" Kai asked.

"Doctor Eklund," Mac corrected himself.

"Oh," Kai replied.

Mac glanced up, but his sergeant's face was studiously blank.

"Keep it to yourself," Mac grated.

"Yes, guv."

Mac straightened, looking around the room. The bag stashed under the bed could be trophies. Either of conquests or simply stolen from female co-workers. He imagined there would be some kind of laundry room somewhere. Maybe Bellamy got off on stealing underwear. That would be the innocent explanation. Blood could get onto clothing in any number of scenarios. But its presence required him to imagine the worst case.

"We need forensics in here," he said decisively. "Get a SOCO team down from…wherever the nearest is. This room will be sealed until it's been examined properly. I'll get some info on Bellamy from Doctor Eklund. We'll let local police know to be on the lookout for him in the area."

"What if he's done a runner? Just headed for the motorway," Kai asked.

"The usual. I'll speak to Reid about getting his description out there. Can't go too heavy. We don't know that he's done anything yet."

"He's been up to something," Kai said, hefting the bag.

Mac went to the door. Taz and Annika were both gone. Mac's lips curled back from his teeth in a brief grimace. He needed to speak to Annika about Gareth Bellamy, and hadn't expected her to just go on about her day. She was prickly. No, more like sharp. Like broken shards of ice. He'd probably offended her by shutting her out of the room. That couldn't be helped. It was a potential crime scene. And her employee was looking more and more like a suspect. Her feelings would have to take a back seat.

"Stay here for now," he ordered Kai. "Once I can get the room locked up, I want to get out there and start canvassing anyone who lives between here and Kingussie. To begin with."

"How big an area is that?" Kai asked.

"Big enough. We'll get the local uniforms on it. Wait for me here," Mac said over his shoulder as he walked away down the corridor.

# Chapter 5

Mac sat down on a bed in a room identical to Gareth Bellamy's. The desk was different, as was the armchair. A few pale patches on the wall showed where pictures had been up for a while, since removed. There was a smell of gloss paint and the windowsill and frames were suspiciously white. The thin, brown carpet looked new as well. Recently set up or freshened up. It was soulless. According to Annika, the staff worked long hours and socialised in the staff room or the local pub in Kingussie. They came back to their rooms to sleep, not to live. She hadn't wanted to spend money on accommodation that would be wasted. Mac wondered if there was something Swedish about that attitude. Or Norwegian, wherever she was from. He bent to untie his boots and kicked them off, then sat back with a sigh. The window looked out into blackness, the forest outside a single homogenous mass of shadow. He and Kai had walked back from the canteen building together and Mac had been struck by the absence of any light beyond the caged, wall mounted storm lights each of the building had.

The sky was black. No stars or moon visible. That pitch dark seemed to flow down to the ground. It was impossible to distinguish individual trees from the black mass beyond the buildings, or the hills that rose on one side. The project was an oasis of weak light in a sea of ink. Mac couldn't remember the last time he had experienced such an absence of light and sound. The occasional growl of a car engine reached in from the A9, but at night that became less frequent. No traffic noise or streetlights was unsettling. Especially once the activity of the afternoon had lessened. He and Kai had spoken to every member of staff about Gareth Bellamy. Mac had liaised with local police to start the search for him and had arranged urgent emails to be sent to all divisions with his description and email details. All under a D-notice for media silence. Although these days that was a hit and miss affair, and down to the relevant editor, as they were only advisory requests and not legally enforceable. The staff had been warned not to talk beyond themselves, but someone always did. Annika and Colin were currently the only ones who knew about the finger. The pathologist had arrived but hadn't been able to shed any more light on what Mac had already deduced. She had taken the body part away for a lab analysis, looking some- what disappointed there wasn't anything more to investigate.

Word would be out already, though. The police were engaged in a manhunt looking for a psychopath who dismembered women and kept their underwear as a trophy. Mac was just waiting for the leak. He glanced at his phone, past ten. Outside, an owl hooted. It made him look towards the opaque window. You just didn't get sounds like that in the middle of a city. It reminded him of Skye. Of roaming the dark moors because he didn't want to go home to his father's drunken rage or the chaos of beer cans and garbage that was his house. His father's house. Not Mac's. It hadn't felt like home since his mother had died. Skye had been as black and silent as this place. Portree wasn't far from the farm, surrounded by an orange glow. As a child, he'd sat at his window watching the lights of cars in town and wishing he were there. Anywhere but where he was.

The screen lit up with a notification. It was Clio.

*You about? Working?*

He replied. *When am I not?* He wasn't, but he'd rather Clio thought he was neck deep in paperwork than sitting and brooding. No sooner had he tossed the phone to the bed beside him than it rang. Mac grinned to himself, not needing to look.

"Hi, Clio."

"Hi, Mac. Close your laptop. Are you still in the office?"

"No. I'm at Kingussie Wildlife Park,"

Silence for a moment.

"Run that by me again." Laughing.

"Yeah, the proverbial fish out of water. Something happened up here, and I got the brown end of the stick. Me and Kai are up here looking into it."

"What happened?" Clio asked, then she spoke again before Mac could reply. "No, don't tell me. I'm not going to talk shop with you. You have enough people to talk about work with."

"Right. How's Yorkshire?" Mac asked.

"Wet and gray. Maia is in love with my dad's sheepdog and even more in love with the beach. We're out every day in the freezing cold."

"Sounds inconvenient," Mac replied.

"It's restful. Kingussie? That's up in the highlands, right?"

"Depressingly high," Mac said.

"Oh, Mac, really," Clio laughed again. "You're in one of the most beautiful and ancient landscapes in Scotland. In the UK. In Europe. It's just what you need, no matter what nastiness you're up there to look into. Fresh air. Peace and quiet. Tell me what you can see."

"Nothing. It's dark and there is literally nothing outside but pitch blackness. It's depressing." Mac complained.

But it was banter more than genuine negativity. That was why he worked so hard to maintain his contact with Clio. Even when she was on sabbatical at her father's house at Flamborough in East Yorkshire. That sabbatical had lasted a month so far and he was missing her. Though not a word of that could ever pass his lips.

"Wow, you are gloomy tonight. Snap out of it, McNeill," Clio said with mock chastisement. There was silence for a beat. "Maia misses you," she said in a more genuine voice.

"I miss her," Mac admitted, able to say it when he was talking about a child.

"I miss you."

"You'll get over it," Mac deadpanned.

Clio chuckled. "Pig."

"Oi!" Mac protested.

Clio exploded into laughter. "Sorry. I meant pig as in man. Not pig, as in copper."

"I'm hurt."

"You'll get over it. So, tell me why you can't switch off even when the distraction of the city is taken away?"

"It just reminds me too much of where I came from," Mac admitted.

Clio didn't answer, and Mac knew why. He'd played the silence card in interviews more times than he could count. It stretched on.

"I can wait all night," Clio said.

Mac barked a laugh. "Skye is very rural. Quiet. Boring. Nothing to do except drink and increase the population. I'm a city guy. I need life around me."

"You've got life around you," Clio pointed out.

"Doesn't feel like it," Mac said. "Feels like I'm in a desert. Nothing to drown out my own thoughts."

"Actually, I know exactly what you mean," Clio said, suddenly serious. "I felt the same when Maia and I got to Flamborough. I'm just not used to it. The silence was deafening."

"Have you had a drink?" Mac asked.

"No. Not that I was an alcoholic or anything," Clio protested.

"I know," Mac replied, evenly.

Clio had been leaning on the bottle to deal with the trauma of the recent past. She hadn't leaned so far that she'd fallen over, but Mac knew it was a steep slope once she stepped over the edge. And it could get vertical real quick. He'd been the one to suggest Clio take a break from her stressful university job. Get Maia a temporary place in a local school and move back with her father. Her mother had died just a few months before, pushing her even closer to the vertical drop it would be so hard to climb back out of. He didn't want to mention her mother to her, not knowing how to talk about it. There was a fear in him that if he mentioned it, she would break. And he didn't know how to deal with that.

"But I've been dry since I came down here. Dad doesn't drink, so it's easy not to. I don't want to set the example to

Maia that a bottle of wine is the answer when you're feeling stressed. Or that it's just normal at the end of the day."

"How's she settling into the new school?"

"Fine. Dad's a governor and the teachers on the whole are a lot more educated about neuro-divergence and additional support needs. So far, it's all shiny and new and she loves it. Art in particular. Dad is overjoyed. She's been painting in his studio with him."

"Your dad's a painter? I don't think you ever told me that," Mac said.

"Didn't I? I thought I had. Amateur only, but I think he's really dived into it since...since mum went," Clio said, a catch in her voice. "God, it creeps up on me. I swear I was OK before I picked up the phone to you."

Mac could hear the tears in her voice, could see Clio scrubbing angrily at her face. She wouldn't want to show so much emotion, particularly in front of him. Clio seemed to sense his discomfort with it. He cleared his throat, not sure what to say.

"You've been through this twice. How did you deal with it?" Clio asked.

That made Mac laugh. "You don't want to take me as an example. I upped sticks and moved to the other side of the country and lived in a bedsit in Gorgie. I was on my way to being a junkie or an alkie. Or both. Someone took pity on me, kept an eye on me."

"Who?"

"An Asian couple owned the flat I was in and the shop it was above. Rayan Ansari and his wife. She made sure I was eating. Then when a bunch of skinheads tried to torch the shop, I jumped in."

"Wow. Like Batman. Maia will be impressed."

"Not quite. I could never get that superhero landing

right. I got a kicking, which would have gone a lot worse had a copper not happened by. Davey Garvey. God, I haven't thought of him for years. He was the one who introduced me to Strack,"

"Strack?"

"DI Laird Strachan. It was Strack that made sure those skinheads got what was coming to them. He was bent, but at the time I couldn't see it. He got justice, and that's what impressed me."

"So, that's how you ended up joining the police?"

Mac sighed, running a hand through his hair. "Aye, it was. And I set about making a complete hash of it under Strack's wing. Almost got me killed."

Clio sniffed, but the catch in her voice was gone. Mac realised that the conversation had distracted her enough that the almost overwhelming upsurge of grief had quietened.

"Seriously though, I don't know how you deal with losing two parents."

"I hated my father and my mother died when I was very young," Mac said, more harshly than he had intended.

He winced at his own clumsiness and hoped he hadn't offended her. Clio's voice felt like a lifeline, a connection to a world beyond the empty darkness he was surrounded by.

"Must have been some emotion when he passed, though, wasn't there?" Clio asked.

Mac considered his words this time and how he said them. "Relief was a big one. Resentment that he'd left me on my own. Fear."

He shrugged, even though she couldn't see it. It was an affected casualness to take the sting out of the emotions.

"I just remember Skye as a dark place. Always dark.

Dark sea. Dark skies and dark people. This place reminds me too much of it."

He was changing the subject, steering it away from his parents, not wanting to go there. The image of his father, as he had found him, swam into his mind. He'd stepped around the chair, propping up the old man's body to pick up a whisky bottle and take a long, burning swallow, looking at the body of William McNeill, decimated by his alcoholism and grief. Death hastened by rat poison and a shotgun to the head. Mac blanked the image out, eyes going to the dark window, trying to draw that emptiness into himself. His stomach was tense, shoulders rigid. He realised that he'd been quiet for a few moments, and so had Clio.

"We're a pair, aren't we?" Clio laughed, suddenly. "Talk about happy campers."

"Your fault. You brought up parents. Now I need a drink. Or a smoke. Or both."

"Don't you dare. I hope you're a good way from the nearest shop."

"I'm a good way from the nearest anything. God, it's the backside of nowhere."

Complaining was easy and he could exaggerate it, make it into a joke. Clio laughed and soon the conversation had moved to the safer sphere of banter between friends. Mac felt himself beginning to relax. A traitorous thought came into his head that maybe the reason things hadn't worked out with Siobhan was his terror of facing his own emotions. Talking about them. It was hard enough with his psychiatrist, Doctor Dan Hendry. It had to be done. He knew that. Just not right now. Right now he wanted to enjoy the back and forth, hear about Maia and Yorkshire. Forget work. Forget Skye. Put Iona from his mind for just a wee while.

She would never be too far away. A ghost half-glimpsed from the corner of his eye.

## Chapter 6

**B**reaking glass. Mac was instantly awake, head lifting from the thin pillow, eyes wide. Had it been in the dream? He stared into the darkness that seemed to have oozed into the room from the window. With the cheap plastic bed-side lamp switched off, the room was as black as a mine shaft. He could just about make out the slightly paler darkness outside if he stared long enough. The sound of wind in the trees was loud, a hushed roar. He realized that the silence he had found so unnerving before hadn't been so complete. The sound of the trees had always been there. Like the rush of cars on a busy city road. Ever present but muted in his mind. There was no repetition of the noise. Nothing but the trees. Just a dream then. He let his head fall back to the pillow, then thumped it in irritation, folding it in half to get more padding. He was used to sleeping with two. A new sound reached him. The creak of a board. Mac went still. The pre-fabricated buildings were wooden framed with felt or wooden shingle roofs and rattling windows. None of the interior doors fitted the frames properly, and they shook with any strong breeze. The floorboards settled and stretched, cracking and making sounds like footsteps.

But this was something else. It was slow, and it moved in a linear way. Like someone treading slowly, knowing the floorboards would creak and trying to move carefully enough that they didn't trigger the worst of them. Breaking glass. Stealthy movement. Mac threw back the blankets and put his feet down. He was in his boxers and t-shirt, jeans on the armchair opposite the bed, shoes and socks beneath. He'd brought a rucksack retrieved from the car after dinner. That was stowed at the foot of the bed. He didn't bother with a change of clothes or his boots. He pulled on the jeans and went to the door. Putting his ear to the wood, he closed his eyes, though it made little difference in the darkness. Somewhere to the left came the sound of a door clicking as the handle was slowly turned and the door pulled open. Mac did the same, moving with patient slowness and managed to be quiet. He put his head into the corridor only, looking first one way, then the other.

It was dark but pale light fell through a window further down, from the floodlight illuminating the car park fifty yards away. A dark shape moved against the dim glow at the far end of the corridor. From the room next to his came the sound of snoring. Kai hadn't been woken by the intruder. Mac watched and waited. It disappeared to the right of the corridor. Mac remembered there was a door there, leading to the laundry room. Cautiously, he crept from his room and approached the door. There were sounds of movement, as though someone was moving piles of washing about. Soft sounds of fabric flumping to the floor. Mac reached the door and cautiously put his head around the frame. A light shone from around a hunched figure. It lit him up enough to reveal combat trousers tucked into boots. Camouflage jacket and a dark woolly hat. Mac recognised the get up even without being able to see the auburn hair. Gareth Bellamy. Breaking into the residential block to do his laundry in the middle of the night. It was ludicrous enough that Mac had to stifle a laugh.

He watched, curious about how this was going to play out. Bellamy straightened, holding something in one hand, shining the torch onto it and then stuffing it into a pocket. A piece of clothing. Not big. T-shirt maybe. Mac reached around the doorframe and felt for the light switch. As Bellamy turned, he found it. The room lit up with a staccato flicker as the strip light stuttered into life. Bellamy blinked and for a moment stared with mouth open. He had a pair of jeans in his hand and a pair of socks sticking out of the same pocket he had stuffed the other garment into. Mac moved to fully cover the door. He saw the instinct to fight taking over Bellamy. The slack mouth, wide eyes, hands dropping to his sides, arms slightly out.

"Don't do it, pal," Mac warned. "You're in enough trouble."

"Get out of the way, copper."

"Not a chance," Mac said.

He had just spotted the long, black shape propped against the top-loading washing machine beside the door. A rifle. Left there as Bellamy had entered the room to free up his hands to search the industrial size laundry basket next to the machine. The contents of that basket were strewn across the floor behind Bellamy. As Mac's eyes took in the gun, Bellamy darted right and got a hand to it, swinging it around with the practiced skill of a soldier. He held it at waist height, barrel pointing unerringly at Mac. One hand held the rifle butt, the other the barrel.

Mac slowly raised his hands but didn't move.

"My sergeant is a light sleeper. I only have to shout. You remember him, eh?" Mac said.

"I wasn't ready for him. He shows up I'll shoot both of you. Get out of the way!" Bellamy hissed from between gritted teeth.

"No, you won't," Mac said patiently.

He leaned against the doorframe, still with hands up, palms outward.

"Your finger's not on the trigger and you haven't shot the bolt. So the gun's empty."

"I loaded it already," Bellamy said.

"I don't think so. You're ex-army? A professional doesn't load and cock a weapon and then climb in through a broken window. Let alone leave it lying around behind him. Come off it, Gareth, do yourself a favour and talk to me."

The light was wavering. Bellamy's face was contorted in panicked anger. The face of a cornered animal. The sound of his breathing was a rapid bellows in the room. Mac affected a pose of relaxed indifference, but he was alert, waiting. The rifle suddenly swung up to the ceiling as Bellamy tried to hold the weight of the rifle entirely in one hand so he could use the other to pull back the bolt and put a round into the chamber. Mac moved rapidly, ducking low and powering forward so that his head slammed into Bellamy's stomach. He had been closer to loading the weapon than Mac had thought. The gun went off, a deafening crack in the confined space. Bellamy crumpled as the breath left him and Mac seized the rifle by the barrel and stock, pulling it towards himself while keeping the barrel pointed up to the ceiling. Bellamy didn't have the strength to hold on. Mac pulled it from him, found the safety and clicked it on before sliding it out of the room along the floor.

He heard heavy footsteps from Kai's room before the door was snatched open and his sergeant was sprinting for the laundry room naked except for a pair of tight shorts. He kicked the rifle, yelled in pain, and then skidded to a halt in the doorway.

"Secure the weapon," Mac barked, hauling Bellamy to his feet by the front of his jacket.

"Thought I was dreaming for a minute there," Kai said. "Where'd he come from?"

Other voices could be heard now. Doors were opening. Mac still held Bellamy firmly, looking him in the eyes.

"No way out, right? So, calm yourself and talk to me."

———

THE STAFF ROOM was repurposed as an interview room. Mac ran the fingers of both hands through his tousled hair. Kai rubbed sleep from the corner of one eye. Mac felt awake in the brittle way that came from being startled out of sleep. His phone sat in the middle of the coffee table, recording. Bellamy sat opposite. Kai perched on a sofa, arms on his knees and fingers clasped. When either of the policemen spoke, Bellamy would be looking at one of them but not both, leaving the other to watch his reactions unobserved. Mac had arranged the room for just that purpose, dragging the table to its centre and the sofa from against the wall to a position on his left. Mac sat back, a steaming mug of coffee in front of him. Bellamy smoked in defiance of the no smoking sign on the door. Annika was outraged at the disruption and Mac thought she blamed him. He and Kai arrived, and all hell broke loose in her well run project.

Mac watched Bellamy. The cigarette was meant to

communicate indifference, but there was a tremor in the hand that held it.

"Why did you run?" Mac asked into a silence that had held for a few minutes.

"Just don't like police," Bellamy shrugged.

"Neither do I. But I don't run away from them," Mac said.

"Not a crime is it?" Bellamy was sullen.

"Assault is," Kai said.

Bellamy's eyes shot to him, then down.

"We searched your room. Found what you'd been hiding," Mac said, hedging with his statement in case there was anything else they hadn't yet found.

A two man SOCO team had arrived from Inverness. Nothing else in the small room had turned up. Fingerprints matched those they had subsequently taken from Bellamy. Samples taken for analysis, which would hopefully produce some DNA.

"Not a crime," Bellamy said.

"What, dressing up in a bird's underwear?" Kai scoffed. "No, mate it's not a crime,"

Bellamy's head whipped round, nostrils flared. Then his eyes slunk back to Mac, and he visibly calmed himself.

"I meet local girls. Go for a drive. Some of them leave their pants in the back of the car. I don't want the next one to find them, do I?"

"Plausible," Mac admitted, nodding. "But that doesn't explain why you broke in and started rifling through your dirty washing."

Kai snorted, and Bellamy twitched. Something about the sergeant got under his skin and Mac intended to exploit that to the full. Kai had been briefed and was gleeful about being the wind up merchant.

"I just needed a change of clothes. Ran out with nothing but what I was wearing," Bellamy answered.

"Get some clean clothes from your room then," Kai said with a touch of incredulity.

Mac spread his hands as though in agreement. The clothes that Bellamy had been stuffing into his pockets were now in clear evidence bags from a box of them Mac had in the boot of his car. Mac picked up one, containing a pair of jeans. They had visible stains on the front of the legs. Dark with occasional streaks of green.

"Unless you wanted to take these clothes specifically," Mac said. "Why would someone be keen to get their hands on clothes they'd put in to be washed before they actually had been?"

"In case someone else got their hands on them first," Kai answered.

Mac nodded. "When these get sent to the lab, what will they find?"

"My guess is DNA," Kai said.

"Mine too," Mac replied, holding Bellamy's eyes. "I've got a dead girl out there somewhere. Doctor Eklund tells me you're a sex pest and you have a collection of female underwear. On top of that you break in to steal your own dirty laundry. Whose DNA am I going to find, Gareth?"

"Those girls are nothing to do with me!" Bellamy shouted, leaping to his feet shoving against the table.

Mac shoved back, rising as well. Bellamy was terrified but Mac wouldn't let him off the hook, held his eyes. Finally Bellamy turned away, going to the window, hugging himself and shaking his head.

"All those girls were consenting. You're not pinning that on me. They wanted it rough, right? That's not rape."

Mac kept up the pressure. He moved around the table

swiftly, backing Bellamy up until the other man was trapped against the windowsill. Mac moved into his personal space, close enough that he could feel his breath.

"I said dead girl and you're talking plural. So you better explain yourself, Gaz, 'cause I've got a probable murder case and you're looking good for it. Unless. You. Talk. Sit down!"

Bellamy did but missed the edge of the nearest chair and ended up sliding down the wall in a heap. Tears burbled to the surface. He looked like a scared little boy. Mac stood over him, not ready to let sympathy take over.

"I didn't do anything wrong. There were these girls in a house not far from here. Escorts. I hooked up with them once. Nice girls. I went back and…and…I didn't do it! This is nothing to do with me. I just went with a couple of prozzies!"

Mac pulled a chair over and sat, leaning forward.

"What happened, Gaz?" he said, finally allowing a shade of empathy into his voice.

"I got my wages. Went back. Been knocked back by that lezzer, thought I would…you know," Bellamy said, scrubbing a hand across his face.

Kai silently went to the pack of cigarettes that Bellamy had left on the table. He shook one out and held it towards Bellamy who took it. He lit it and puffed, long and hard. Then held it between thumb and index finger, hand hanging over his knee.

"The car was there when I got there. Big BMW SUV, white. Isabella's car. So, I knew she was in. Thought she was in."

Mac held back from asking questions. The words were pouring out of Bellamy now. He looked disheveled, like he'd been hiding in the woods since running. He was cold, wet, and probably hungry too. And riven with fear. Now his defences were down and the story gushing forth. Mac didn't want to interrupt the flow.

"The front door was open. Like, just open, ajar. I knew then that something was wrong. Should have just legged it. But I went in. There was blood everywhere. They'd been shot."

# Chapter 7

**D**unachton House. It lay on a burn that ran under the A9 and into Loch Insh. A convoluted, winding road led to the house, following the gorge that the burn had carved out. Trees lined the precipitate slopes of the gorge on top of slabs of bare rock. They'd had to exit the A9 two miles north and back track along an unnamed b-road until they reached a hump-backed stone bridge crossing the Dunachton Burn. It was barely large enough for Mac's car. Bellamy was under uniformed guard back at the wildlife park. A police van lead the procession. Mac's vehicle was sandwiched between the van and a marked police car bringing up the rear. Kai was in the van, navigating the convoy through the maze of tracks and back roads. Bellamy had been knowledgeable enough about the surrounding country to point to the house on a map.

Two women shot dead. Possibly a third by the name of Isabella. Bellamy didn't know her surname. He'd described her as in her mid-40s, blonde and busty. Just the kind of woman he liked. And he'd been left under no illusion that she would cut his balls off if he looked at her the wrong way. She was in charge of two girls who were at Dunachton House for the purposes of being rented out. Whether or not by their consent was unclear. Bellamy wanted it known that nobody had been coerced when it came to him. The van turned right onto an even smaller road, climbing steeply and winding as it rose. At the top was the house. It looked expensive. A collection of squares with tall sheet glass windows and walls of timber. Modern architecture and built as a bespoke project for its owners. This wasn't Taylor-Wimpey, or a restored crofter's cottage. This place reeked of money. The windows were dark and the front door open. A white SUV sat on a gravel drive in front of the house.

The van stopped, and the back doors opened. A tactical team came out and deployed themselves around the property. Kai exited from the passenger side and ran to Mac's car, keeping the van between him and house, running in a crabbed crouch. Mac pulled in beside the van and the remaining police vehicle turned across the entrance to the drive, blocking it. Both uniformed cops inside got out through the driver's side, one man clambering across the car to do so. They crouched. Kai got into Mac's car, radio in hand. Over the open channel, Mac could hear the tactical team communicating with their commander. A flurry of negative replies came over the crackling radio. No sign of life. No sign of a shooter.

"Looks all clear outside the property, sir," the tactical commander said.

"Proceed inside," Mac instructed.

He and Kai got out and moved up to the rear of the van looking around the back of the vehicle towards the house, keeping low and not presenting a target to any potential sniper inside. The black shapes of the tactical team, torches mounted on the barrels of their guns, were slipping into the house. The lights cast by those torches swung in short, stabbing motions as the guns were swung back and forth, quartering the area.

"In a hallway. Stairs ahead. Rooms to left and right. Blood. Watch your feet!" came the tactical commander. "Large room to the left, sofas and a TV on the wall. Fireplace. More blood."

A succession of all clears began to sound.

"Downstairs secured, sir."

Mac waited.

"Upstairs clear. Two bodies, one in a bathroom at the rear of the house, other in a bedroom."

Mac straightened and walked towards the house. He'd taken shoe covers and gloves from his car and was putting on the gloves as he walked. Before entering the house, he slipped on the shoe covers, knowing that there was no way to preserve the scene perfectly because of the clumsy feet of the tactical team. But as there was a witness to a gun crime taking place, Mac had no choice but to allow the tactical team to go in first. He would have been content taking his chances and going in alone. Once upon a time, anyway. Now, he found he was happy to wait for the all clear. That was a change in him for sure. Approaching the front door, the coppery tang of blood was indisputable. He slipped through the open door without touching it. Blood was sprayed up the wall to the right of the door and there was more up the stairs. He recognised the splatter pattern made by a gunshot, probably to the head. To the left was another room. Switching on a light switch with a gloved hand revealed what looked like a living room. Luxurious white furniture, leather. Large flat-screen TV on the wall and an ostentatious marble fireplace.

Thick carpet and wallpaper across three walls, patterned brightly and featuring a busy design. The fourth wall was a different design. A so-called signature wall. It was a jarring contrast, but Mac suspected it had cost a king's ransom. Furniture, wallpaper, and carpet were all ruined by blood. It looked like a massacre had happened here. Mac didn't do more than give the room a cursory look from the doorway. It was difficult enough to avoid the blood on the hardwood floor of the hallway. In the living room, the thick carpet would have soaked it up, creating a red swamp. He skirted a large, congealed puddle on his way to the stairs. There, he followed a diagonal path around the blood, careful to avoid touching the stained walls. Members of the tactical team were still positioned around the house, where they had checked every room. Mac picked his way around them.

The decor here was pale, favoring natural tones. It made the blood even starker. A trail led along a carpeted landing to a large bedroom. A queen-size bed was dwarfed by the overall scale of the room with a high, sloping ceiling and inset windows. Mirrored, built-in wardrobes reflected Mac from across the room. Floor to ceiling windows had thick curtains closed across them. Lights were set in the ceiling and showed a naked woman on the floor. She was face down, hands by her sides. She had thick dark hair which was matted with blood at the back of her head. Mac carefully maneuvered his way around her. Then he walked back to the hall and looked down the stairs. An armed officer looked up at him curiously. He nodded to Kai, who clicked the radio.

"Withdraw the tactical team," he said.

Those on the upper floor carefully moved to the stairs. The order was echoed by the commander and soon Mac and Kai were alone in the house. Mac descended the stairs halfway. There was a splatter pattern against the wall to the right of the door as you entered. High velocity gunshot from someone standing opposite, in the doorway of the living room, perhaps. Streaks of blood against the wall of the staircase and mashed into the carpet. Someone dragging themselves up the stairs. Halfway up was a distorted handprint. Someone stumbling as they climbed, putting out a hand to steady themselves.

"Someone was killed at the foot of the stairs by a person already in the house," Mac said.

Kai looked, taking in the chaos of blood, and just nodded.

"Possibly they came downstairs, turned to face the living room and bang. Body was left at the foot of the steps. That accounts for the concentration of blood down there. At least one wounded person came upstairs."

"Why? You do that and you're just cornering yourself. Why not make a break for the back door? Try and get out?" Kai wondered aloud.

Mac had the same thought. He slowly walked back up to the bedroom and looked at the dead woman there. Blood soaked the floor beneath her and not just around her head. There had been a bleed somewhere around her torso too, at the front, no sign of wounds at the back. Her hands were smeared with blood and the nails, where he could see them, were broken. The trail of blood led to her. She had crawled up the stairs, dragged herself up, leaving her life blood behind her. Why? He walked out of the bedroom and into the hallway. There were more doors leading off it and he tried a few. At the end of the hall was a bathroom. Another girl. Lying on her side, a smear of blood on the claw-footed bath beside her. Bullet hole in the middle of her forehead. Her head faced the door.

"Gunman enters the property. Shoots someone to the right of the door. Shoots and wounds another woman before proceeding upstairs. The wounded woman follows. He goes into the bathroom. Surprises this one. Shoots her in the face. Turns around and goes down the hall. Shoots the previously wounded woman, his third victim, in the back of the head in the bedroom, where she's managed to get to. What made her go upstairs after the killer?"

"She wanted something. Maybe she had a weapon up here and wanted to try and kill the gunman before he got her?" Kai suggested. "Or maybe revenge?"

"Or she knew that this woman was up here and wanted to protect her. Which would make these two close. Maybe even family."

"Think these are the two escorts Bellamy was talking about?" Kai asked.

"Probably. We'll find out soon enough. But, by my reckoning there's a body missing," Mac said.

"Maybe the splatter downstairs came from one of these two."

Mac shook his head. "Forensics might say different but I only see one major wound each that could cause a head height splatter like that. One of them lived long enough to crawl upstairs. If the splatter came from this one," he glanced back at the woman on the bathroom floor. "Why bring her up here, and risk contaminating yourself with all that blood?"

Kai looked bleakly from the bathroom, down the hallway. "You like Bellamy for this?" he said skeptically.

Mac was staring at the dead girl. Under all that blood,

she might have been pretty. Her body was slim and well-toned. He shook his head. "This took a psycho. Bellamy's not on the same level. I think he found this house of horrors and panicked. That's why he ran when he realised the polis had turned up. Thought we were here for this."

"And his clothes might have their DNA on them," Kai suggested as they both left the bathroom.

"If these are the escorts, then yes. Or at least one of them. Maybe both."

"What a stud," Kai muttered darkly.

"I want him put through the wringer. Everything about this blood bath he can tell us, including Isabella. If she's a pimp, then she knows who they are, where they're from and who arranged to bring them here."

Everywhere Mac looked, there seemed to be wall-to-wall blood. It was as hellish a place as he had seen in his time. The smell of it was rank in the air. There was something obscene about seeing the normality of a place next to the aftermath of such carnage. A picture on the wall untouched and unstained. A toilet roll on a holder. A paperback on a bedside table. Reminders that this was a house, perhaps a home. Designed to make people comfortable and happy within. And it had become a scene of utter devastation.

"This all remind you of anything?" Mac asked as they descended the stairs.

"I don't know. Hostel?" Kai asked.

"What?"

"It's a movie. Never mind, guv."

"It looks like a hit," Mac said. "Someone comes in and methodically kills everyone in the place. No attempt to disguise it. And if this was a brothel then it belongs to someone much higher up. Someone with money."

"Christ. You don't think this could be connected to the war between John Lowe and Hance Allen?" Kai asked, realisation dawning.

Mac shrugged. "We'll keep our minds open but this is one Musa isn't getting his hands on."

# Chapter 8

Brunswick Street, Edinburgh South-East Division headquarters. Home for Mac, probably for more hours than his actual home. Turning into the private entrance, he saw the Police Scotland sign outside had been defaced. Again. He smiled. He could hear road works in the distance and everywhere he looked was concrete. The day before, he'd been surrounded by trees and unable to sleep because of the god-awful smothering silence of nature. That and the complete absence of light. Now, he could smell exhaust fumes, bins, and hear the noise of human progress. And he had what was looking like a triple murder to solve. He got out of the black Audi he'd bought to replace the one he'd totalled during a panic attack, running a red light, and putting himself and his passenger, DI Barland, in hospital. The door clunked closed in exactly the same way the last one had, in a very satisfying way. He thought about the encounter he'd had while in hospital from a concussion because of that accident. Siobhan had been the attending nurse. She must have transferred from Pediatrics to A&E since they broke up. And she'd seemed...sympathetic. If he was reading her facial cues correctly, which wasn't always a given.

He swiped into the building and pressed the button for the lift directly opposite the door. He hadn't pursued it. She'd offered to be there if he needed to talk. One thing had led to another. A case. Another case. Before he knew it, six months had passed, and he hadn't called or text her. Neither had she. But that felt more distant now. A couple of years ago, he would get excited at seeing an old text from her, thinking it was a new message. Now...as the lift carried him to the fifth floor, Mac very deliberately put thoughts of Siobhan from his mind. Siobhan and Clio. Except, he hadn't been thinking of Clio until that moment. He shook his head, running a hand through his hair, straightening the lapel of his dark suit jacket. His uniform. By the time the lift doors opened, his face was still and his mind was clear.

Pushing through the double doors onto the SCU floor, he saw the cluster of desks that had once belonged to DCI Akhtar. No longer an SCU officer. Transferred after a case review into two of her cases. Both found to be unsafe. Mac had found the perpetrator of both crimes. It must have been salt in the wound for Akhtar. She was connected. Had been connected. Deputy Chief Constable Mayhew probably didn't return Akhtar's calls after his neck had ended up uncomfortably close to hers. Now those desks were used by a team three times as big. DCI Benjamin Musa had two DIs under his command, each with a sergeant and five constables. They filled the available space and turned the open floor plan into a humming bustle. Musa hadn't wanted Akhtar's glass fronted office though. The head of the Organised Crime Taskforce had a sixth-floor office next to the Division Commander. They'd both attended

Glasgow Uni and probably exchanged the same secret handshakes.

DI Mel Barland was in before Mac. As always. Being a new mum hadn't slowed her down. First in the office, though she couldn't hold a candle to her boss for late nights. A slender woman with long, curling red hair and petite features was talking to her. She looked around as Barland smiled over her shoulder at Mac.

"Morning, guv."

"Morning, Mel. You must be Isla," Mac greeted the new face.

She stood and put out a hand. "DC Isla McVey, sir. Good to meet you. I'm…"

"Liaison with the supercop," Mac finished for her.

Her brow creased in genuine puzzlement. Mel shot Mac a warning look. He smiled disarmingly.

"Sorry, just what your guvnor gets called behind his back. Could be worse names."

"Yes, I suppose. He does get quite a bit of media attention."

"You're looking at the champ in that regard," Mel said, nodding to Mac. "The media loves our boss. It's those smouldering good looks and baby blues. They can't get enough of him."

Mac grimaced. "Alright, Detective Inspector. You've had your thirty seconds of piss take. Let's get to work, shall we. I've got a real horror show for us."

"You want me in on the briefing guv? I'm only supposed to be liaison over the Kelly and Grant cases."

"Yes, stay. Musa wants you over on my team for the time being, and I'm going to need all the bodies I can get. I need to talk to Reid first. Then I'll brief you both."

Mac hung up his overcoat on a hook behind his office

door and, hands in pockets, went back out, along the corridor to Reid's office. He rapped twice and opened the door without waiting. Reid was flicking through a sheaf of paper. Mac recognised his own report on the Kingussie case. Reid was glowering, shifting in his seat like he had trapped wind. Finally, he dropped the papers with a sigh and fixed Mac with a jaundiced glare.

"I send you up north to look into some dumb tourist who fell into an enclosure at a safari park and got munched. You bring me two murders and a missing person."

"I got lucky," Mac replied, poker-face.

"What the hell is going on?" Reid replied.

"A woman going by the name Isabella is likely our missing person. 40s, blond and buxom apparently. She isn't one of the two corpses. They were too young. We still don't know who they are. But a witness says a woman called Isabella was staying at the house. The house has been searched and there is nothing in there to indicate anyone's identity, which is suspicious in itself. Almost like someone was making sure there was no way of knowing who lived there…"

Reid raised a hand. His face had gone still. Mac frowned as Reid wiped a hand across his eyes. Suddenly, he looked exhausted. Reid had always looked like a bloodhound. Now, the pouches under his eyes, the extra chin, and jowls beneath all seemed to sag, tugging his mouth down at the corners. He looks like an old man, Mac thought. A tired old man. It was a shock. Reid had always been a vital presence. A crusader. First going after his colleagues as part of Anti-Corruption, then as superintendent of a team of detectives in Serious Crimes. Now he looked beaten.

"I know who she is, son," he said. Then he swore.

Mac paused, the automatic recitation of memorised

facts, resetting himself mentally. He stretched out his long legs, crossing them at the ankle, and folded his arms. An instinct told him that whatever was coming next, he wouldn't like it.

"So?" he said.

"Isabella North is an American citizen who has lived in this country for about ten years. Now holds a UK passport as well. And her boyfriend goes by the name of John Lowe."

Reid held Mac's disbelieving stare. Then Mac laughed aloud, but there was little humour. He sat forward, elbows on knees and both hands combing through his dark, unruly hair.

"Shit," Mac said.

"Tell me about it," Reid replied.

"How did you know?"

"Would you believe he reported her missing this morning?" Reid said.

"No," Mac replied.

"You had breakfast yet?" Reid asked.

"Yes."

"I haven't. Come on."

Reid got up and strode out of his office, squat and rolling in his gait. Hunched shoulders and white hair. Mac followed him down to the lift. They rode it in silence and then walked to Mac's car. Reid went to the rear passenger door. Mac grinned ruefully as he clicked it open and Reid got in.

"You can be the chauffeur," Reid said.

"Where do you want to eat?" Mac asked as he started the engine.

"Have a day off, son, will you? Just drive for a bit, eh?" Reid snapped.

He didn't put on his seatbelt but sat staring pensively out of the window as Mac chose a random direction to drive in. Edinburgh crawled by arteries clogged with rush hour traffic. The pavements were busy as they headed north towards the Old Town. Black sooty stone buildings alongside hideously ugly eighties replacements. Ultra-modern architecture was poking up here and there like exotic weeds. Streets twisted and turned seemingly at random. Unlike Glasgow which had been deliberately designed around a grid shape, Edinburgh's road system was a brachial mass of branchings and connections. Tarmac gave way without warning to rattling cobbles and back. Bus lanes appeared without warning. Mac loved it.

"Going to brief me then, sir?" Mac said.

"I got a call from John Lowe in the wee hours this morning. On a burner phone, a courier brought to my door and took away with him after the call. His girlfriend Isabella is missing and John thinks it's another attack on him. First his business, then his personal life."

"By Hance Allen?" Mac asked.

"That's what he thinks, son. And he wants her found, and it stopped."

"Understandable," Mac said.

"Is it, aye? Glad you're so bloody empathetic all of a sudden," Reid snapped.

"It had the look of a mob hit, that's all. Violent and ruthless. I have someone being held at Inverness on charges of assault, but he's not a viable suspect for the killings. We might find some women willing to come forward with sexual assault charges right enough. But he's not got this kind of crime in him."

"I've read through your requisition requests and your report. I've authorised the lot. Extra bodies in the field, mobile HQ, and lab facilities up at Kingussie, helicopter coverage. The works. This is top priority for us now, Mac."

"I know," Mac said. "Is that because you got a call from John Lowe?"

"'Course it is. Christ, it's no wonder I promoted you to DCI, is it?" Reid snapped.

He was in a fine mood today. Mac remained silent. They passed the castle on their right and high above, working their down through Grassmarket. The buildings were tall and closely packed. It was a concrete and brick forest.

"He thinks he can wind me up and send me off to do his bidding," Reid continued. "Wants police resources to fight his war for him. I need to make it seem like I'm going along with that. But, I'm not. Because I see an opportunity to get out from under John Lowe's thumb, right?"

Mac nodded, seeing what Reid was getting at and why he was so keen not to be overheard.

"You want to fit him up," Mac said.

"I do, son," Reid replied with satisfaction. "Now, a little bird tells me that Isabella was involved in Lowe's business. She wasn't just a trophy girlfriend. She was a business partner too."

"We have some anecdotal evidence that our two dead girls were prostitutes and Isabella was the pimp."

"Right. So, suppose she was doing the dirty on Lowe. Trying to rip him off or sell him down the river to our old friend Hance Allen? What might he do to her, eh?" Reid said, leaning forward.

"Suppose there is a war started by Allen," Mac said. "Musa thinks so."

Reid swore long and hard, bringing a slight twitch of a

smile to Mac's face. Reid didn't care for Supercop any more than Mac did.

"If Musa proves his case against Allen and brings my case into it, which I think he'll try to," Mac said. "There's not much I can do about it."

"Make it happen for me, son. This is my one chance to get clear of him." Mac glanced into the rearview mirror.

Reid's voice had been full of supplication and it was an emotion that Mac wasn't used to hearing from him. Looking at his boss he was once again struck by how old he looked. And tired.

"Maybe you should get out while you can, sir," Mac said, softly. "You're no use to Lowe out of the force."

Reid shook his head. "Maybe not, son, but I'd also be a nobody. In this world you either have power or you don't. If you don't you're at the mercy of those who do. I'm just not ready to be one of the little people. Callum…"

Mac knew he was in trouble when Reid used that name. His given name. A name used so infrequently he sometimes forgot he had it.

"Callum. This is the last favour I'll ever ask you for. Do this for me and I'll make sure you're the one replacing me. I need him to go down for this. Whether or not he did it."

## Chapter 9

"**Y**ou're in a lot of trouble, pal," McNeill said.

Gareth Bellamy stared back, wisps of steam curling in front of his face from the polystyrene coffee cup on the table. A man with slick, sculpted dark hair and a professionally blank expression sat next to him wearing a gray suit. He looked young for a solicitor but Mac thought that was probably more to do with his own age. Everyone looks young these days. Bellamy snorted, picking at the edge of the plastic table. Pale daylight spilled into the room through high up frosted glass windows reinforced by a mesh of wire. The scared boy who had broken down at Kingussie in front of Mac and Kai was gone. Bellamy had become braver after talking to his brief. He didn't have a solicitor of his own so the young well-dressed man was a duty solicitor arranged by the custody sergeant at Inverness Police Station. Mac's eyes felt gritty. He'd opted to drive up and had started out at four in the morning. Melissa sat next to him, annoyingly bright-eyed. He took a sip of awful coffee, black as petrol.

"I didn't do it," Bellamy finally muttered. "Can I have a fag?"

"No," Mac replied. "Didn't do what, exactly?"

"What you're trying to fit me up for," Bellamy replied.

"No-one's trying to fit you up, Gareth," Melissa said reasonably. "You're here because you're a legitimate suspect in a murder enquiry."

"We found DNA on your clothes belonging to both of the women found dead at Dunachton House. A place you admit to visiting," Mac said.

He reached for a plastic bag on the table and brought it directly between himself and Bellamy.

"Your DNA was found at the house in several places but notably the bedroom where one victim was found, we're calling her Victim A. And in the bathroom where another victim was found. Victim B."

On cue, Melissa opened a folder and produced two glossy, full colour photographs of the dead women, placing them deliberately in front of Bellamy. He pushed his chair back from the table, looking away.

"Specifically, old traces of your semen were found on the bed," Mac said. "So could you tell us who either of these women were? And what your relationship was to them?"

Bellamy glanced at the brief who nodded.

"I don't know who they were. They were escorts. I told you this already," Bellamy said. "I went to there to hook up."

"How did you know there were two escorts at Dunachton House?" Melissa asked.

Bellamy looked at her with scorn that made Mac grit his teeth. "I went online. I know where to look."

"And where is that?" Mac asked.

"A website for escorts. I've used it before. Two new girls were up on the site and they were local. Couldn't believe my luck."

"Bet you couldn't," Mac grunted. "Who runs the site?"

"How should I know? All I do is I pay a deposit and I get an email telling me where and when. I pay the rest when I arrive."

"Cash?" Mac asked.

"A Cash App. I call when I arrive and get an email telling me to pay the rest."

"Who's the email from?" Mac persisted.

Bellamy shrugged, picking up his coffee cup and sniffing it before putting it down. "Don't know. Just a mailbox. The only person I've ever dealt with was Isabella. Yank. She answered the door and gave me the ground rules. Real hard-faced cow."

It made sense to Mac. There was deniability throughout the process. If caught, Isabella could claim she knew nothing about what her house guests were up to and there was nothing tying her to prostitution. No cash. No digital audit trail. Just anonymous mailboxes and burners for any phone contact. The only thing tying Isabella North to the property was the presence of her car and Bellamy's statement that a woman called Isabella had greeted him. The house could be a rental. But a rented property wouldn't be as secure for this kind of business. There would be an owner somewhere who might want to inspect or sell. It would make more sense if this house was owned outright. But not by any name that could be traced back to the real owners. Probably a shell company owned by another shell company. Plenty of insulation in case the police came knocking. He'd set Kai trying to find an owner but so far no luck.

"When did you last visit Dunachton House?" Mac

asked, looking to lever a reaction out of Bellamy by the sudden change of topic.

"Friday night," Bellamy said after a glance at his brief and a nod from him.

Mac and his team had arrived at the wildlife park on Saturday afternoon. Mac nodded slowly.

"And tell us what you found," Melissa said.

"I've already told you this," Bellamy said, clasping his hands together on the table in front of him. "I've given you my statement,"

"Tell us again," Mac said, tonelessly.

"Is that necessary, Detective Chief Inspector?" the solicitor asked. "My client has already given a written statement which covers this."

"And I want to hear it again," Mac told him.

Bellamy sighed, putting his face into his hands.

"I'd arranged to be there at seven. You've got my phone, so you've seen the emails. I paid my deposit before I left and then drove over to the house. I got there and emailed to say I was waiting. I didn't get a reply. Isabella's car was there, and the lights were on inside the house, but I didn't get a message to tell me to pay."

"How many times had you done this?" Melissa asked.

The interjection was rehearsed. Something to break Bellamy's flow, make it harder to recite the same story word for word.

"Once before," Bellamy said.

"So how long did you wait?" Mac asked, talking over Bellamy's answer.

He got flustered for a second. "About ten minutes, I think."

"Then what?" Mac leaned forward, closing the gap between them.

Bellamy leaned back, the response Mac was looking for. It showed that Bellamy was uncomfortable, which meant he was off balance. Again, more chance of catching him in a lie.

"I went to the door. It was open."

"Open as in unlocked? Or actually standing open?" Melissa asked.

"Actually open. I could see into the house. I saw the blood. So I legged it."

"No, you didn't," Mac said, sitting back. "Because you told us those two women had been shot."

"Ok, ok! I went in. I went upstairs, and I saw Sofia…"

"Who?" Melissa interrupted.

Bellamy was bright red and rubbing sweat from his upper lip. In his written statement, he'd denied knowing the names of the women. He'd stated he didn't care. It wasn't important to him what they were called, only what they were willing to do.

"May I have a moment with my client?" the brief said, diffidently.

"Which one was Sofia? The one in the bedroom or the one in the bathroom?" Mac asked.

"I only saw Sofia. She was in the bedroom," Bellamy said.

The solicitor leaned in, but Bellamy waved him away.

"I didn't do it!" he snapped. "I found Sofia, and I legged it. Went back to the centre, to my room and I didn't see or talk to anyone. I used a couple of prostitutes. I didn't kill anyone!"

"I'll let you speak to your brief, pal," Mac said. "Let you get your story straight."

He stood, and Melissa announced the suspension of the interview for the tape. Mac left the room, followed by his DI. They went into the room next door. Melissa switched off the mike that would allow them to hear the legal advice Bellamy was getting. Mac would have left it on. Kai was sitting with Isla McVey in two plastic chairs in front of the mirror. The room was small, cramped with all four of them and smelling strongly of Kai's aftershave. The two of them had spent the morning showing Bellamy's picture around Kingussie and Aviemore, looking for anyone who might know him. They were trying to build a picture of the activities that had resulted in Bellamy's collection of underwear. They had arrived at Inverness after Mac and Melissa had gone into the interview room with Bellamy.

"What have you got?" Mac asked, leaning against the edge of the table.

"He's definitely been making a pest of himself locally. A few waitresses and barmaids recognised him," Kai said. "None of them had a good word for him. Said, he was a sleaze. One or two admitted to going on a date with him."

"Anyone hinting at sexual assault or rape?" Melissa asked, skimming through notes as she spoke.

"No-one's coming forward so far," Isla said. "We had one man in Aviemore who would like some time in a locked room with him. He runs a holiday park. Seems his eighteen-year-old daughter, Stacey Mulligan, went out with someone and came back in tears with a bruise around her neck. He couldn't get a name out of her, but one of her friends showed him a picture on a dating profile."

"Did she make a complaint?" Mac asked.

Isla shook her head. "Too ashamed. I asked if I could talk to her but she's gone to stay with grandparents in Aberdeen. On another subject, I emailed the address Bellamy said he used to arrange his escorts. Just to see if

85

there was still someone monitoring that mailbox. Haven't had a reply but got a read receipt, so someone has seen it."

"Could be that Isabella isn't the one who ended up being fed to the wolves," Kai said.

"We'll find out soon enough. Her partner is on his way up here to identify the ring," Mac said. "Might be worth using that fact to see what else we can shake out of Bellamy," he said to Melissa.

Mac was sure that Gareth Bellamy wasn't the killer he was looking for. Resisting arrest while carrying a firearm didn't make him the cold-blooded killer that had turned Dunachton House into an abattoir. That took the ability to divorce yourself completely from empathy or conscience. Bellamy was a misogynistic prick who was certainly capable of violence against women. But what Mac had seen in that house was a different breed. The solicitor had got out of his chair and walked to the mirror, tapping on it once with a knuckle and then giving a thumbs up sign. He was young and clearly assumed that Mac was going by the book and therefore unable to hear him.

"Come on," he said to Melissa, heading for the door.

In the interview room, he waited for Bellamy, or the brief, to speak. It was the solicitor who was the first to break the silence.

"My client now realises that his initial statement contained some omissions and wishes to set the record straight to avoid confusion and to prevent police time being wasted," he said.

"Nice of him," Mac replied.

Bellamy remained silent. "He previously denied knowing the identity of the woman whose dead body he discovered. He does, and he also knows the name of the other woman, Katya. He knows no more about them other than that they had Russian sounding accents. He is no expert and cannot say that it is Russian as opposed to any other eastern European country. Somewhere in that part of the world. He omitted this information previously out of fear but now wishes to do all he can to assist your inquiry."

"Tell us about Stacey Mulligan," Mac said as soon as the solicitor had stopped talking.

Bellamy's head came up. His eyes were wide and his hands planted against the edge of the table as though preparing to push himself back from it. Again the solicitor looked at his client and Mac raised a hand.

"Don't ask us to leave the room again. I've got my steps in for the day. Just tell me what you did to her."

"I didn't do anything," Bellamy said, spit gathering at the corner of his mouth.

"Her dad thinks you did. There were marks on her throat and she was hysterical. Her dad wants to get his hands on you and he won't be the only one. So talk to me."

"Detective…"

"I asked him, not you!" Mac snapped.

"Help us understand what's been going on," Melissa said, reasonably. "There's a missing woman, two dead women and now a girl in Aviemore who you went out on a date with and came back hurt and terrified. Do you see how this is looking?"

"I really must insist on time with my client," the solicitor said, more forcefully.

"You're trying to fit me up!" Bellamy shouted, eyes wet.

"I don't think you did it. Not what happened at Dunachton House. You need to convince us you're not lying though or you'll never convince my guvnor. Or the Procurator Fiscal," Melissa said, smiling in a motherly way.

"Look. I've got a way with the girls, OK? I can pick up

girls. And I like, you know, some rough stuff. Stacey said she was into it but then she panicked and started crying. I threw her out of the car and left her. I'd barely touched her. She still had her knickers on for Christ's sake!"

The solicitor had actually put his face in his hand, increasingly frustrated. Bellamy was in full panic mode. Mac wished for an earlier era in which he could have thrown him around the room for a bit. He was in a rush to confess to attempted rape to get off the hook for a triple murder. It made Mac feel sick. He folded his arms, watching the terror on Bellamy's face.

"Why don't we draft a new statement that covers all the relevant facts, shall we?" Melissa said, pushing a pad and pen across the table to Bellamy.

"What do you want me to say?" Bellamy said, looking at Melissa with wild, glances to Mac.

"Start with the names of the all the girls you've been taking underwear from," Mac said. "Cover meeting Sofia and Katya. Anything you know about Isabella."

"I've told you all that. I wasn't lying. I know their first names. I barely spoke to Isabella. She just told me the rules. I can't remember the names of the other girls…"

"Try harder. You know who Isabella North's boyfriend is?" Mac said, slapping the table and making Bellamy jump and give a small whimper.

"No," Bellamy stammered.

"His name's John Lowe. He's a gangster from Edinburgh. A pretty evil one, too. And he's on his way up here to see if it's his bird that ended up being lunch for a wolf pack. Trust me; you do not want this guy thinking you're the one responsible, Gareth,"

"Ok, ok, ok. I'll tell you everything I know. The names are all in my phone. I honestly don't remember…"

"We'll get you your phone. Jog your memory. Melissa, you can run the rest of this interview."

"Right, guv,"

Mac left the room, Melissa announcing the fact for the tape. As the door closed, he heard the solicitor vociferously protesting. He didn't care. Bellamy was a lowlife, and he was going to do time, probably for sexual assault. He'd suffer inside, but Mac couldn't feel any sympathy for him. In his mind, he couldn't help but picture Maia, a few years away from Stacey Mulligan's age. The idea of Maia being taken advantage of by a predator like Gareth Bellamy enraged him. Then there was Iona. Outside the room, he stopped for a moment, staring at the tatty noticeboard. Dog-eared leaflets were pinned up there, listing descriptions of stolen goods and motors alongside rotas and shift change requests. He pulled open the door of the observation room next door.

"Someone go and sit in with Mel," he said, putting his head through the door.

He walked away along the narrow corridor towards a coffee vending machine at the end, hands thrust into trouser pockets. Inside, he seethed with the need to inflict violence. He knew that unshackled by duty and the law, there would be nothing to stop him from beating a lowlife like Bellamy to a pulp. Some people didn't need laws to prevent them from doing things like that. Mac understood his own anger well enough to know that he wasn't one of them. A dirty window next to the vending machine looked out over a car park and a grey river under a steel sky. Rain dotted the glass, and he ran through his mantra silently, acknowledging the trauma and letting it wash over him.

## Chapter 10

**M**ac sat in a waiting room supposedly designed to be comfortable but succeeded only in looking dated and bleak. A gray sofa with rings worn into the arm from countless mugs was the main piece of furniture, along with an armchair in the same colour but not the same shade. A coffee table held a glass vase of flowers that gave the only spark of colour. Walls and carpet were institutional, muted and neutral. There wasn't a window, and the lighting was rendered diffuse by the ceiling panel that covered it. It looked cheap and felt depressing. Mac didn't think John Lowe would care. He put the plastic container, holding the ring, down on the coffee table and was about to take a seat when there was a knock at the door. A uniformed constable opened it and looked at Mac, a question in his eyes. The answer was a sharp nod. The constable stepped aside, and John Lowe entered the room. Entered the room and filled it.

He was a small man but stocky. Head was shaved bald; a line of stubble marking where it had receded to before he'd got rid of it all. His forehead was lined and his blue eyes sharp. He wore a white shirt open at the collar and a pair of jeans over white trainers. Gold glittered on his fingers and at his wrist. The overcoat he wore was rendered more luxurious in its appearance by being so casually matched with jeans and trainers.

"So you're him?" Lowe said, looking at Mac.

"DCI McNeill," Mac introduced himself.

"I know. Reid told me about you."

Lowe looked him up and down. There was a different air about John Lowe compared to Hance Allen. Allen was an old hand, probably wearing the same suit he'd bought thirty years before and spending his time in the same boozers he'd been drinking in since he was eighteen. Lowe looked like money. Mac knew Lowe lived in a centuries old manor house somewhere out Queensferry way, with its own grounds and golf course. A year or two earlier, Mac would have said that Lowe was a backstreet gangster without the legitimacy that an old hand like Allen had built up. That had changed quickly. Changed enough that coppers like Benjamin Musa were now paying very close attention.

"Is that it?" he said, nodding towards the plastic box.

"Yes," Mac said, reaching down to remove the lid and pick up the ring within.

Lowe took it, his face giving nothing away as he turned it over.

"Aye, I recognise it. It's the engagement ring I bought for Izzie. The stone's unique. No other like it in existence," Lowe said.

He closed his hand around it and put it into his overcoat pocket.

"I'm going to need that back," Mac said.

"Why? You've had your forensics going over it. You're

done with it. It's my property," Lowe said, turning to the door.

"John, its evidence. I can't let you walk out with it," Mac said.

He hadn't moved but Lowe turned as though Mac had grabbed his arm.

"John, is it, aye? John. You've only just met me, pal. You might think you know me, but you really don't. I'm taking it. Speak to your boss, Kenny Reid, if you're not happy."

Those cold blue eyes held Mac's, but Mac neither blinked nor looked away.

"Give it back," he said, calmly. "I'll give you a receipt for it."

Lowe barked a laugh, turning fully to face Mac and stepping towards him, closing the gap between them quickly. Mac didn't move, but he put out a hand for the ring.

"Your boss expects handouts from me as well," Lowe said.

"That right?"

"It is right. You're not on the books yet, are you? That can be fixed. Everyone's got a price."

"The ring, John," Mac said.

"You call me that one more time and we're going to have a falling out," Lowe said quietly, but loaded with menace.

Mac felt a rebellious urge to call him on his threat, but had the sense to keep quiet. Nothing to gain from provoking the man too much. Just enough to let him know Mac wasn't intimidated.

"Very good. You're learning," Lowe said and put the ring into Mac's hand. "We done, yeah?"

"No. I need to talk to you about your fiancée. Take a seat."

"Without a brief?" Lowe said, sitting in the middle of the couch with legs planted apart and hands clasped between them.

"This isn't a formal interview. Just a chat about your missing fiancée," Mac said, sitting in the armchair.

"Right. You want a recent picture?"

"I have one. Taken from the CCTV in a shop in Kingussie with two friends a week ago."

Mac took a blown-up photo from a folder that had been sitting on the coffee table beside the plastic box holding the ring. He turned it around to show Lowe. It revealed a woman with blonde hair tied back. She wore a white track-suit that revealed her midriff and white and gold trainers. Two dark-haired women were visible behind her.

"That's handy," Lowe said, barely glancing at the picture.

"Any idea who her friends are?" Mac asked.

"Nope," Lowe replied, not looking.

"Try looking at the picture," Mac said.

Lowe smirked, glanced down. "Not a clue. I didn't know any of Izzie's friends. We weren't that kind of couple."

"What kind of couple were you?" Mac asked.

"What does that have to do with the price of fish? She's missing. Find her."

"I found her ring," Mac pointed out, knowing that Lowe would be fully aware of exactly where it had been found.

"If your next question is going to be, how did it end up there, you're asking the wrong man. Izzie left to come up here a month ago. That was the last time I saw her."

"And where was that?" Mac asked. "The last time you saw her."

"At a golf club dinner," Lowe said.

"Which one?"

"Royal Troon. I flew out there with Izzie by helicopter. Not mine sadly. Not quite that rich yet," Lowe said with a grin.

"When?"

"The seventeenth of last month," Lowe replied without hesitation.

It was well rehearsed. He knew what he wanted to say and had no compunction about telling the truth. Because it could be easily checked. No point lying.

"We stayed at the Crown Hotel in Troon," Lowe said. "And I flew back to Edinburgh the next day."

"Where did Isabella go?" Mac asked.

"She was meeting friends who were flying into Glasgow. Then heading up here for a break."

"Funny time of year to have a holiday in highlands," Mac commented.

"She was a funny woman," Lowe replied. "Desperate to show off the highlands to her friends."

"Where were they from?" Mac asked. "Not here, obviously."

"Not a clue. I didn't know them," Lowe said, rolling his eyes. "I'm starting to feel like I need a brief. And a proper interview room if you're going to keep asking me questions. I don't need the soft furnishings."

Mac leaned forward in his seat. "I noticed that, John. You're different from the grieving spouses I usually see in situations like this. A man thinks his wife has been fed to the wolves, usually finds that upsetting, eh?"

"I've had a hard life," Lowe said. "Makes it tough to show emotion. Inside, I'm crying."

Mac noticed the smallest change in the other man's

expression. An additional hardness had crept into an already hard face. Lowe's thumbs were fidgeting, tapping against each other. Mac decided to push it.

"I know those two girls were prostitutes. Probably trafficked here for that very purpose. And your fiancée was their pimp. That's why they were brought here."

"Did they say that?" Lowe asked, thumbs suddenly still.

"No," Mac said. "Because someone killed them both."

By Lowe's face, Mac might have talking about the football scores.

"That's a shame," Lowe replied. "I had no idea."

"When did you realize Isabella was missing?" Mac said.

"When she didn't call me like we'd arranged she would," Lowe said. "We always call each other. Even when we're apart. And we often are. Work, you know?"

Mac nodded. "When had you arranged to speak?"

"Thursday night," Lowe said. "Last Thursday,"

"Yet you reported it on Monday to DCS Reid?"

"I was busy. I text her a few times over the weekend. Got nothing back. The messages were being read, so I thought she'd taken the huff with me."

"Why? Had you fallen out?"

Now Lowe sat forward, running a be-ringed hand over his bald head and smiling.

"Now, I'm really feeling like this is an interrogation, which is not on unless you've read me my rights and given me the chance to phone my brief."

"I'm sorry to be so clumsy at this difficult time," Mac replied, coldly. "What did you argue about?"

Lowe stood suddenly, then stopped. He tugged at his shirt cuffs, revealing the gleaming stones in his cufflinks. He cleared his throat and then smiled.

"The last message I sent to her was on Sunday night,

about six. It's been read. So, someone has her phone. Here, this is mine. You're welcome to use it if it helps. I've unlocked it."

Mac stood and reached for the phone. He had no doubt that Lowe wouldn't hand it over unless it had been forensically cleaned. There would be nothing incriminating on it, but he was intrigued by the notion that someone was reading the messages on Isabella's phone. Not Gareth Bellamy. He was in a cell downstairs, bricking it. Lowe didn't let go of the phone immediately. He held Mac's eyes, fingers tightening on the device.

"Nothing incriminating on there. To me," Lowe said, quietly.

Then he let go and grinned.

"Nice meeting you Detective Chief Inspector. I think we're going to work well together. What do you think?"

Mac produced an evidence bag from an inside pocket, one of a number he kept folded there.

"To find your fiancée. I hope so," he said.

"Nae, beyond that. My business is all about relationships, you see? That's how I've got where I am. Building relationships," Lowe pointed from Mac to himself. "I can spot a relationship that's going to be important to my business. And this is one."

Mac picked up on the undertones. It was a veiled threat. Not of violence. Nothing so simple. The threat that Lowe might find a lever that would put Mac in his pocket.

"Everyone has their price, that about it?" Mac said.

"Aye, something like that," Lowe said.

He turned and left the room. Mac weighed the phone in his hand, wondering what it contained. Nothing that could incriminate Lowe. But, maybe someone else. Reid? He would need to look through it before handing it to a digital forensics team. Even Kai, his own digital specialist, couldn't be trusted if there was anything on there linked to their boss. Mac was confident in Kai's loyalty to him but not Kenny Reid. He wouldn't put any of his team in that position. Slipping the phone into his inside jacket pocket he put the ring back into its box and left the room.

## Chapter 11

There was a mobile HQ set up in the grounds of the private section of Kingussie Wildlife Park. Several Police Scotland branded Portakabins had been brought in by HGV, along with their own generators, lab equipment, computers, and portable toilets. There was even a kitchen area with a microwave, a kettle, and a fridge full of anything that could be zapped hot in five minutes or less. Cupboards were stacked with dehydrated noodles, pastas, and macaroni along with crisps and biscuits. Coppers ate worse than builders. There were Scottish Transport Police stations in Inverness and Dundee with facilities, but Mac didn't want his team to be that far away from their crime scene. Or scenes. It was still unclear where Isabella North had been taken. Hayley Blackwood had been brought out to look at Dunachton House. Mac had wanted Derek Stringer, but the Edinburgh-based pathologist had refused point blank to travel up to the highlands. Not unless he was heading up there for a grouse shoot had been his words. It was way out of his jurisdiction, so Mac couldn't insist. Not that he had any reason to doubt Hayley Black-wood's ability. He just disliked novelty.

By the time he'd returned from Inverness, she was waiting in the HQ cabin, drinking tea with Melissa. Hayley was tall and slender with a strong jaw and dark hair cut to frame her face. Her eyes were dark and with a slight tilt that made her look to be mixed race. South-east Asian. She was pretty. Mac couldn't quite place her age. From her face, she might have been anywhere from mid-thirties to his own age. She glanced over as he opened the door. The cabin was wide enough to accommodate a row of desks along one wall, each bearing desktops and monitors. Mac had a desk at the far end. The windows along one side looked out onto the gravel and broken concrete of the car park. Annika Eklund's pre-fab labs and accommodation were on the other side. Hayley stood and put out an eager hand. She wore a dark trouser suit that robbed her of gender and gripped his hand firmly as she shook it.

"Detective Chief Inspector. Your name precedes you. I'm looking forward to working with you," she said.

"Thanks," Mac grunted, not the best at accepting flattery.

Her skin was smooth, and he could smell the faintest whiff of a subtle citrus perfume. Just a hint of femininity from a woman clearly working hard to fit into a predominantly masculine workplace.

"You've been through the house?" he asked, nodding for her to take her seat.

He put hands into his trouser pockets and leaned on the edge of the nearest desk. He hadn't been present when Blackwood had first come down from Inverness to examine the finger. Kai had been his liaison. Mac hadn't felt pathology could tell him much that wasn't already evident.

Having met Hayley Blackwood, he thought Kai would be cursing his luck that he'd been assigned to follow up on John Lowe's story about Isabella going to Glasgow Airport. Still, he was in the company of Isla McVey, so couldn't complain too much.

"I have, my team and I have been processing it since about six this morning," Hayley said.

She turned to a laptop on the desk behind her and unlocked it, bringing up a series of colour pictures.

"You can link up to the projector over there," Melissa suggested.

There followed a minute of cables and plugging in, followed by Melissa closing the blinds on the windows and switching off the overhead strip lights. The projector on the desk at which Hayley was sitting shone on to a whiteboard on the far wall. Mac found himself looking at a succession of familiar images. Blood spattered walls, carpets, and furniture.

"Two different weapons were used," Hayley began. "We found no shell casings anywhere in the house. Which means they were found and picked up by the killer. But the pattern on this wall which is located to the right of the front door as you go into the house, just at the foot of the stairs, indicates a head shot from a high-velocity weapon."

Mac nodded, glad to see his own instincts had been spot on.

"We found fragments of skull and hair against the wall to bear out this hypothesis. The pattern of blood gives an indication of the velocity of the bullet though without casings we can't confirm type."

"You didn't find bullets either?" Mac asked.

He had realised that the wall over which the blood was splattered showed no sign of a bullet hole.

"A high velocity round would surely pass right through and bury itself in the wall, wouldn't it?"

"It would and did. But the bullet was removed," Hayley said.

She clicked the laptop's track pad and brought up an enlarged, magnified image of a neat circular hole in the wall.

"This was difficult to spot because of the blood and tissue that had run down the wall and effectively filled and covered it. The hole is larger than a bullet would make and it's solid wood, not plasterboard. The killer dug it out."

"That took some time. Very cool," Melissa said.

"Planned," Mac said. "And by someone with a good idea of exactly how much time they had."

"The bullet had been dug out of the torso of the body found in the bedroom. A large, wide-bladed, and very sharp knife with a partially serrated blade was used. A hunting knife probably," Hayley said, showing a picture of the woman Mac now knew was called Sofia.

"The body in the bathroom had been killed with a headshot. The mirror was shattered. From the fractal pattern of the remaining broken glass, I would say it was hit by the bullet that killed her. Then dug out of the wall, which caused two-thirds of the glass to fall. You can see the enlarged hole in the wall here."

Another picture. Close up and showing a rough circular hole with a few shards of glass clinging to the surrounding wall.

"What about DNA?" Mac asked.

"Obviously the two women. Four more DNA sources were found. Three in the form of semen with matching DNA found elsewhere as skin cells, hair follicles. Enough material to indicate three separate men had been to the house and engaged in some kind of sexual activity while there."

"And the fourth?" Mac asked.

"Unknown. Found traces all over the house. I would say it must be someone who has lived there or at least spent a lot of time there. The three male sources are primarily centred on the bedrooms, bathrooms and living room. Visitors I surmise who came into the house, were entertained with drinks in the living room then went upstairs."

"That bears out what we know of the two women," Mac said.

Hayley looked at him questioningly.

"We believe they were prostitutes," Mac explained. "So you're saying I potentially have three customers coming into the house at some point and a fourth person possibly living there. Plus, these two."

He pointed at the screen which now showed Katya lying in the bathroom.

"Yes, the separate DNA sources would bear that out," Hayley said confidently.

Mac was beginning to forget his misgivings about having a new pathologist on the case.

"What evidence do you have that two different guns were used?" he asked.

"The fact that the shot to the torso lodged in the body. I would say a handgun was used for that shot. I'm not a ballistics expert, but I was an Army medic before I retrained. So, I'm familiar with what different weapons can do. I would say your killer entered the house and fired a headshot from the hip with a rifle to make his first kill. The victim had already descended the stairs, presumably after hearing the door open. Their back was to the wall on the right side of the door when the shot was fired. The exit wound was higher at the back of the head than the entry wound, indicating a weapon held like this."

She mimicked holding a rifle with both hands and angling it up from her hip.

"Which would be a very good shot," Mac said. "Difficult to make a headshot even at close range with a hold like that. So, he walked in and immediately shot woman one through the head with a rifle. Then he switches to the handgun for the second shot, hitting woman two in the stomach. Not immediately deadly, but incapacitating."

"Why switch though?" Melissa wondered aloud. "Must be awkward indoors."

"Maybe the rifle jammed?" Hayley suggested. "Or he didn't have time to turn and point the rifle at the second victim. He pulled it quickly from his waistband or holster and shot the second victim as he swung round. It would explain why it was a stomach shot and not the head. Perhaps she surprised him?"

"Possible. Or else they lost the first weapon. Maybe there was a struggle with the person coming down the stairs," Mac suggested. "Anything in the evidence to support that?"

"Nothing so far. No indications of blood belonging to anyone but our three gunshot victims," Hayley said. "But there's a lot of blood at this scene. Always a possibility that a drop or two belongs to our gunman. Sorry, gunperson. Male chauvinist bias."

"I don't mind. I'm not a feminist," Mac said.

"With two-thirds of your team made up of women?" Hayley said with a playful smile.

Mac missed the emotional content and heard only the words.

"I pick the best officers regardless of gender," he said, seriously.

Leaning forward he reached for the mouse and clicked back through the slideshow of pictures frowning in concentration. Hayley looked to Melissa who gave a shrug and a faux grimace. Mac missed it all and when he looked back at them both had schooled their faces to stillness.

"So, this is looking like a professional hit. Planned in advance. Our killer appears to have known how many people were in the house and how long they had to clean up afterward. No wasted or wild shots. A marksman even when things went wrong, and they were forced to switch weapons. Am I missing anything?"

"Yes," Hayley said. "Drops of blood on the driveway. I wanted to present the evidence in chronological order based on what I believe the sequence of events were."

She took the mouse from Mac, her slender fingers resting on his momentarily. Mac removed his hand, folding his arms. But his eyes found Hayley's and held them for a moment. There wasn't the hint of a smile on her face but she bit her lip slightly. Melissa was looking up at the screen.

"Here," Hayley said, finding the relevant picture.

It showed dark spots which had been circled in yellow paint, a numbered marker placed next to each.

"There's a trail of them. We know that at least two people left the house. Presumably the killer with a body. We've used your onsite lab facilities here to match the blood types. These drops were from the same person who was shot at the foot of the stairs."

"Where does the trail lead?" Mac asked.

"Into the trees where it becomes impossible to follow."

"I'll get onto the nearest K9 unit," Melissa said, turning to her computer, fingers already dancing over the keyboard.

"Good work, Doctor Blackwood," Mac said.

"Please, call me Hayley," she replied with a bright smile. "This is a really interesting case. When Melissa told me your usual pathologist is Doctor Stringer I was really excited to work with you. He's pre-eminent."

"Is he?" Mac smiled. "He's always struck me as a grumpy old toff."

"Oh no, not at all. He gave lectures when I was studying for my degree in pathology at Napier. Always happy to answer questions. He was a lovely man."

Mac chuckled at the idea of Derek Stringer as a cuddly old codger with a twinkly eye and a kindly smile. It didn't fit the grumbling, rotund man with a taste for the finer things in life and contempt for anyone who couldn't trace their family tree back to the Stuarts. He found himself glad that Stringer had not been willing to take a trip into the highlands. This close to Hayley the perfume was more evident, and she was biting her lip again, glancing at him from under her lashes. Mac was dimly aware of Melissa talking on the phone and stood, hands in pockets, and moved over to her. Hayley began disconnecting her laptop and Mac stole a glance at the long, slender lines of her legs in the trousers that became tighter fitting when she sat with legs crossed. Melissa hung up.

"We're in luck. There's a mountain rescue team at Laggan which maintains a dog team trained for search and recovery. They can have dogs and handlers with us in a couple of hours."

Mac nodded. "Doctor...Hayley, I'd like you there with us in case the dogs find another crime scene."

"Yes, of course. I've got a change of clothes in the car."

# Chapter 12

**M**ac had brought a change of clothes in his own car. When word was received the mountain rescue team was a few minutes from Dunachton, Mac changed into jeans, fleece top and boots in a cramped toilet. As he emerged, he was smoothing back ruffled hair with a quick finger brush. Hayley Blackwood was sitting sideways on the driver's seat of her car, a small red hatchback, lacing up a pair of serious looking hiking boots. Macs were well broken in by virtue of weekends spent at country parks with Maia and Clio. He had a rucksack containing some forensic clean gear, evidence bags, and torches. He glanced at his watch, the same digital watch he'd been wearing since Siobhan's daughter had bought it for him as a birthday present. He'd stopped wearing it for a while when he realised how much it reminded him of happier times with the two of them. But the angst he'd once felt every time he looked at it had burned away. Now he wore it because it was practical to wear a watch. The people attached to the memories were from a different chapter of his life. Numerous pages had turned since that particular time. The story had moved on.

The sky above was grey. A wind found its way through the trees that felt like it had come from a fridge. Mac zipped up the fleece and then his all-weather jacket over that. There were gloves stuffed into one of the pockets but he hadn't thought to bring a hat like the woolly one Hayley was tucking her dark hair into. It emphasized the shape of her face and contrived to make her look prettier despite the wool bobble dancing about on the top.

"We can take my car. Over there," Mac said.

Hayley got into the passenger side, putting a rucksack of her own at her feet.

"I've got some sandwiches and a small flask as well as a field kit. Hopefully, this trail won't take us far enough to need it."

Mac considered that as he drove back towards the A9, heading north towards the cutoff that led to Dunachton House. He had assumed the trail would be short. A man or woman carrying the dead weight of another adult couldn't have got far, surely.

"I'm hoping you won't. I think we'll find a trail leading to a track where something with four-wheel drive was parked. Then the body was moved cross-country to the edge of the wolf enclosure and dumped for them to dispose of. It seems convoluted, but we know the wolves got hold of a part of the body somehow. It's the most logical explanation."

Hayley nodded thoughtfully, biting at her lower lip as she frowned. Mac had thought the gesture flirtatious but now wondered if it wasn't just a habit she had. He put his mind away from her looks and concentrated on finding the turnoff he was looking for.

"Do we know who our dead body was?"

"Yes, I believe it's a woman called Isabella North."

"Do you know her size and weight?"

Mac shook his head. Finding the turnoff, he steered the Audi into it. He stopped as something off to the side of the road caught his eye. A small, dark car was parked in a layby just after the junction with the main road. He drew up the Audi alongside and wound his window down. The car was empty. It was a small SUV type, four doors and slightly higher than a regular car. A Nissan. A popular make that could be seen in their millions in the UK. Mac wondered at it being there, given that Dunachton House was cordoned off. The trees grew close to the layby, undergrowth clustering to make getting out of the passenger side difficult. No obvious paths that Mac could see, but then maybe hikers made their own. He pulled forward until he could see the registration plate in his rear-view mirror, then he took out his phone and called Melissa.

"Run a reg for me," he asked, reading out the vehicle's number plate phonetically. He waited a minute or two while Mel ran a search.

"Registered to Neill Smilley, lives in Nairn, on the coast not far from Inverness, I think."

Mac thanked her and hung up, driving on.

"You think it's related?" Hayley asked.

"I don't know. Mr. Smilley might just be having a day in the great outdoors. Merely coincidental that he picked a spot on the way to our crime scene."

"I did some reading on some of your cases after you called me out to look at the finger," Hayley said as the car wove its way between damp, canyon walls. The burn burbled and thrashed along beside them.

"Oh, I didn't realise they were public knowledge," Mac said.

"There's a lot in the media about you. Certain true crime threads on Reddit among other places. And I have access to path reports."

"Right," Mac said, not liking the idea of his cases being discussed by true crime nuts.

"Some really interesting cases," Hayley said.

"Murder's murder," Mac replied.

"Yeah, but a stabbing outside a pub on a Friday night is a bit different from the cases you've investigated. They were a lot more dangerous."

"They've panned out that way. Chances are I won't get another interesting case for the rest of my career. Just kids stabbing each other or drunks giving each other a kicking outside a pub."

"Would you like to talk about them sometime? After work?" Hayley asked.

Mac glanced at her. She was just looking away from him, biting her lower lip again. He faced the front again as her head turned toward him.

"I don't much like the thought of spending my spare time rehashing old cases. The drink, on the other hand... you have anything else you'd like to talk about?"

He glanced a second time. Caught her looking and allowed the rogue's grin an outing, just a flash.

"Maybe," Hayley drew the word out. "Not much interesting about you apart from your cases but I'll give you a shot."

Mac barked out a laugh. They had been winding uphill and now rounded a bend which ended up at the police cordon around Dunachton House. A uniformed officer undid the tape to allow them entry to the grounds. Another directed them away from the path, which had been marked out by forensics. Mac pulled up next to a Land Rover. A man with a thick brown beard and the well-used all-weather gear of a professional mountain climber was standing by it while another was bringing two dogs out of the back. They jumped and panted and barked as they stretched their legs. Mac didn't know the breed, but they were large and rangy, with scruffy coats and lolling tongues. He walked towards the two men.

"I'm DCI McNeill," he said introducing himself.

"Cameron Tovey," said the man with the beard. "Cairngorms Mountain Rescue."

His accent was pure Shetland, an odd lilt to Mac's ear.

"This is Jake McIntosh, my colleague. And this is Burt and Harry. Two of our rescue dogs."

Hayley was out of the car and making a fuss of the two dogs, kneeling beside them, and laughing as they playfully assaulted her. Mac introduced her.

"Did my DI brief you on what we need your help with?" Mac asked.

"Aye, finding a dead body."

"From a blood trail leading from a house into the woods. Can they do that?"

"From a blood trail?" Jake piped up. "These two will follow it to Land's End, as long as it doesn't go through water. Speaking of which we're in for a dose of rain so we'd better get started before your trail washes away."

He had a rugged face, square jawed and lined as though from too many hours exposed to icy winds and pelting rain. He squinted out at the world like Clint Eastwood. Mac nodded.

"Lead the way. Hayley can you show them where the blood starts?"

Hayley led the way towards the house, dogs, and their handlers in tow. A sudden noise made Mac turn. It had sounded like something moving in the bushes in front of the cars. There was no sign of movement when he looked though. He was about to look closer when he reminded himself that woodlands were prone to noises in the bushes. There were probably a million pairs of eyes watching them at that moment. He hurried to catch up. Burt and Harry were sniffing furiously at the blood trail where it began near the front door. Then they were at the end of their leads, hauling their handlers behind them and following the line of forensics markers unerringly. For a moment, Mac thought they were literally just going from bright yellow plastic tag to bright yellow plastic tag, not following the scent at all. But as they neared the edge of the clearing in front of the house, the dogs plunged into the trees without hesitation. Cameron and Jake followed, moving aside whip-thin branches, and shouldering past larger clumps of foliage. They barely seemed to break stride. Hayley followed and Mac brought up the rear.

The light dropped sharply as they moved deeper into the woods. The trees shutting out most of the daylight. Mac quickly began to sweat. The air was close despite the wintry conditions and the pace set by the dogs was brisk, to say the least.

"Someone's been this way carrying something heavy," Cameron called back over his shoulder.

"There're deep prints here and there where the mud's thickest and a lot of branches bent and broken higher than I would expect if it was just one person on foot."

Mac looked but couldn't see anything. Cameron had slowed and was pointing to a tree about four inches above Mac's head. Hayley was looking with curiosity.

"I see what you mean. Either someone very tall or maybe someone carrying another person on their shoulders."

She was measuring, with her hands, the space between her own shoulder and the broken branch. Mac saw it then. For that branch to be broken, Hayley would need to be about a foot taller. For him to break it, four inches would be needed. But someone of his height with a body slung fireman's style over his shoulder…

They trekked on, the ground uneven beneath them, which forced an exhausting rhythm to the march. Mac found himself constantly twisting and shifting to avoid low branches or step around up thrust roots or stones. Mud sucked at his boots without warning, breaking his stride. At other times, he stumbled as the toe of his boot hit hard earth or rock where he'd expected softer ground. The way was tending upwards and the trail being followed by the dogre was very straight. Through his discomfort, cold but sweating, muscles aching and fighting a sense of claustrophobia, he reasoned the killer knew exactly where he was headed. It was too direct a path to be otherwise. They came to a halt on the brow of a hill. The ground fell away steeply in front of them before rising again on the far side of a narrow, choked gorge. Following the line of the ridge opposite, a tall metal fence was visible. The dogs were milling around, no longer certain of a direction. They whined and snuffled, circling back to their handlers.

"Looks like this is where it ends. There's some blood here," Cameron said, pointing to a spot next to a tree.

Mac went over. In between protruding roots was a matted mass of moldering leaves. They were covered in a sticky, reddish brown mess. Hayley knelt, removing her bag, and taking out gloves, a plastic dish, and tweezers.

"I would say the body was put down here for a minute or two. Long enough for blood to be transferred to the ground."

She picked at the mass and placed a couple of pieces of woodland debris, blood-soaked, onto the dish before screwing on the lid.

"That must be the wolf enclosure, down there," Mac said. "Would have been difficult to get down and then up the far side carrying a dead body."

"Nigh on impossible," Jake commented. "With a dead weight on yer shoulders? Nae, I cannae see it."

"Do either of you have binoculars?" Mac asked.

"Aye, here," Cameron said.

He produced a folding pair from a pocket on his thigh. Mac trained them on the lowest visible part of the fence. Then he slowly traced them upwards, tracking along the boundary.

"Can't see any signs of a break in the barrier," he said.

As he reached the highest point, losing sight of the fencing, movement closer to him caught his eye. He swung the binoculars towards it but only saw a blurred green mass. He adjusted the focus until he could see again. There was nothing except trees and plants. He lowered the binoculars, conscious how useless they were at closer quarters. For a moment he saw nothing. Then it was as though his eyes adjusted to the layering of leaves, branches, and trees. Through the confusion he saw the human form in a dark green, oiled jacket. He was crouching down the slope with his back to Mac and the others and had a camera in his hand.

"Hey, you!" Mac shouted, taking a few steps down.

The man looked back over his shoulder suddenly and Mac got a glimpse of a face shadowed by a baseball cap.

113

Then the figure was sprinting uphill, in a direction away from Mac.

"Police!" Mac shouted. "Stop!"

Christ! When had that ever made a running person stop? He took off in pursuit, trying to maintain an angle that would intercept the photographer. It was possibly just an innocent rambler, but they had chosen an odd spot to take pictures. The man stumbled as much as he ran, but so did Mac. Finally, the photographer's feet slipped out from under him and he crashed onto his side, sliding down the slope for a few feet. Mac changed direction and charged down towards him, but also slipped. He got hands under him to keep him upright and bounced off a tree trunk before catching hold of the man's collar and sliding into the muddy leaf mulch beside him. The man was slim and young, looked to be in his late twenties. He started thrashing, trying to pull free and regain his feet at the same time.

"Keep still, you eejit," Mac said. "I'm polis, right?"

"I'm not doing anything wrong. This is assault."

"You'll know what assault is if you don't pack it in," Mac growled. "If I find pictures of Dunachton House on that camera we'll know if you were doing something wrong or not. Who are you?"

Mac released his hold and got to his feet, balancing himself on the slope. He was conscious of Hayley watching from above and Cameron thumping his way down after Mac, Jake stood next to Hayley with the two dogs in hand.

"What if I do? Is this a police state? What about freedom of the press?"

The man's accent was highlands. He fished an ID card with a lanyard wrapped around it from an inside pocket and practically shoved it into Mac's face.

It was a staff ID for the Highland Times and stated his name as Neill Smilley.

## Chapter 13

Smilley sat in the back of Mac's car, looking exceedingly disgruntled. His phone and camera were in Mac's possession, though he knew he was on shaky ground holding them. The trouble was, so did Smilley. He'd gone along with accompanying the policeman back to Dunachton, given that he had strayed onto a crime scene. But once there, he'd wanted to be allowed to go on his way and Mac had no intention of letting him wander off. Hayley was walking towards the car with a smile and a plastic case swinging by her side. She got in next to Smilley, a uniformed police officer on the other side, and began to talk. Mac glanced up and saw the softening of Smilley's sullen, militant expression. He sneered inwardly at how easily the guy was turned around by a pretty face. Hayley wanted a prick of blood as a DNA sample and to eliminate Smilley's blood from the other samples taken at the house. Mac watched as Smilley nodded and put his hand out obediently. Mac looked down at the camera. It was digital. Smilley was a journalist, not a professional photographer.

Mac had the controls down in a minute, switching it on and finding the folder in which recent pictures were being stored. He soon came to a series of shots of the fence.

Several were extreme close-ups, and the camera had managed a better job than the binoculars. Mac squinted and frowned, wondering what he was seeing. Then it became clear. He strode towards the car and got into the driver's seat.

"What am I looking at here, Neill?" he asked.

"That's my property," Neill said, reaching for the camera.

"It might be. Or it might be evidence. It's up to me. Tell me why you're taking blurry, close-up shots of the fence?"

Neill licked his lips and glanced at Hayley who was occupying herself putting away the sample she'd just taken. The copper next to him was stony faced and looking out of the window.

"It's a gap in the fence," Smilley finally said.

The words came out grudgingly. Like he disliked talking to the police, in principle. Mac wondered if he should let Hayley conduct the interview and was surprised at the smallest flash of jealousy.

"Thank you," he said. "Do you know what's on the other side of the fence?"

The answer would be yes otherwise why take the pictures in the first place.

"Of course. Doctor Eklund is trying to reintroduce wolves to the UK. That's why I'm here."

"Looking for a story about Doctor Eklund and her project, I get it," Mac said, trying to show he was on Smilley's side. "What I'm interested in is how long you've been here and how you knew this gap was there?"

"I've been here for about a week on and off. I asked for

an interview with Doctor Eklund. Didn't get one. Got talking to Colin McCauley at a pub in the village and got some info. One time I went for a hike to map the perimeter."

"When was that?" Mac asked.

"End of last week. Thursday and Friday, couldn't do it in one day so tackled the western half first and then eastern section the next day."

"And that's when you noticed the break?"

"No. It wasn't there. I'm sure," Smilley said.

Mac frowned. "That's a helluva distance to cover. How can you be sure?"

Smilley squirmed in his seat, looking frustrated. He sniffed and glanced at Hayley. Then at the uniform who had turned his stolid gaze from the window. He was a big lad and Smilley actually tried to shift away from him a few inches.

"I can't. But I was looking for it. For anything. There's no angle to a story about a scientific plan to bring back their legacy species," he made the annoying gesture of air quotation marks around the word legacy. "But there's a lot of legs in a story about the EU putting money into introducing dangerous animals into our countryside. Instead of in their own backyard, you know? So I was looking for something wrong."

"Enough to cut a hole in the fence?" Mac asked.

"No! You're not pinning criminal damage on me. Scotland is free to roam. This isn't private property. I'm entitled to look around," Smilley insisted.

"You are. I believe you," Mac said, levelly, holding Smilley's gaze.

For a moment the journalist seemed to consider something, he muttered to himself and then deflated, his bravado leaving him.

"I'm willing to help. I'm not hiding anything. I saw something on Thursday night. No, wait. It wasn't Thursday. When were Rangers playing?"

"You mean the Scottish cup match, against Brechin? Tuesday night," the uniform said.

"Was it? Tuesday? Ok, it was because I was listening to the match on Radio Scotland in my car. It was out by this old church on the west side of the enclosure. I was just checking out the roads, seeing how close I could get without having to hike, deciding if I wanted to do this. Got that far and saw a man going into the church. I got a picture of him. Here."

He reached for the camera but Mac held it away from him. "Just tell me, eh?"

Smilley sat back. "I can't remember exactly where I saved it. The camera's getting full. I had to do some moving stuff around."

Mac pressed a back button, and the display screen came up with a list of folders. The number of files contained in each folder was in three figures each, and there were dozens of folders.

"OK," he sighed, handing it over. "Show me."

As he held it out, Hayley shifted in her seat, opening the door, and putting the strap of her bag over her shoulder. She jarred Smilley as he leaned forward to take the camera and it was knocked from Mac's hand.

"Sorry," she blushed a bright red, dropping her bag and reaching down where the camera had fallen into the passenger footwell in front of her.

After a few seconds of trying to extricate it from the narrow space, she produced it and handed it to Smilley.

"I better get this sample back to the lab so we can eliminate Mr. Smilley," she said.

"Right," Mac said distractedly as Smilley hunched over the camera.

"Lay on a car to take Doctor Blackwood to the mobile HQ," he told the PC.

The uniform got out and walked over to the nearest patrol car with Hayley.

"You remember what he looked like?" Mac asked Smilley.

"Difficult to be sure. The light wasn't great. Think he was wearing camo gear, and he had a big backpack. Looked like a soldier. Big guy. Even at a distance, I could tell he was over six feet and built like a tank. Christ, where the hell is it?"

Mac watched him with increasing impatience.

"You've lost the picture?" he asked.

"No! I just can't remember where…wait! I know. I moved it to the SD card."

His thumbs scrambled over the on-screen controls and then froze. He sat back and looked up at Mac with a distinctly nervous look on his face.

"It's gone," he whispered.

"What is?" Mac asked, flatly.

"The SD card. I don't believe it! Look, there's nothing in the slot. It was there before, I swear it. I'm not trying to hide anything!"

Mac breathed slowly and didn't look away from the man in the back. Nor did he speak. Smilley's militancy had evaporated. Maybe he was now feeling that he couldn't prove he wasn't up to something dodgy quite as easily as he thought.

Smilley turned the camera towards Mac, pointing to a slit in the side. There was a small button next to it, protruding from the body of the camera. Mac reached out and pushed it, feeling no resistance and presuming it would be accompanied by the card being ejected had it been there. He took hold of the camera by the lens and took it from Smilley.

"You'll get a receipt for it Mr. Smilley. This has just become evidence."

———

FIRST PRIORITY WAS to secure the hole in the fence. As a matter of public safety as much as part of a murder investigation. Mac dropped Neill Smilley at his car and instructed him to report to Inverness Police Station to give a full statement under caution. If he did a runner, Mac would make sure several books were thrown at him. Mac continued back to the wildlife park and interrupted a conference call that Annika Eklund was hosting. She looked up from her computer screen as he rapped briefly on the door of her office and then immediately entered. She wore a headset with a mike and looked at him as though he had just shot one of her precious wolves. Mac smiled his most roguish grin, which died a death against Annika's glacial cool. She clicked something on the screen.

"Detective Chief Inspector, I'm on a very important call…"

"I've found how the wolf enclosure was penetrated," Mac said. "There's a hole in the fence. I need your help to pinpoint it on a map."

Her mouth was open, and she closed it with a snap

before clicking something else and standing, casting the headset aside.

"You're serious," she said.

"Of course I am. I need your wolves out of the way so I can take a team of officers and forensics in."

Friendly hadn't worked with Annika, and the situation had now become urgent. So Mac had kept his tone strictly unemotional and professional. Annika looked at him for a long moment, then nodded sharply.

"OK, let's get on with it. Good work Detective Chief Inspector. I didn't think it would be the police who would find the break in the fence. It had to be there, of course."

She went to a cabinet and pulled open doors revealing shelves filled with rolled paper. Selecting one, she spread it on top of a metal filing cabinet. Mac saw the familiar outline of the enclosure.

"There's the A9 and this must be the road that runs to Dunachton House. The fence had been breached where it climbs a hill, quite steep. We were on the slope of another hill overlooking it. With a stream at the bottom of a deep gorge in between," Mac was quite pleased with his description of the woodland landscape. Given that most of it all looked identical to him.

Annika was staring at the map with blue, unblinking eyes. "Around here I think. This is where that house is. You can see the road terminating there. This stretch of fence climbs steeply and there's a burn marked too. How far along is the hole?"

Mac had Smilley's camera in his pocket. He opened up the screen and located the close up. Scrolling to the next picture showed the same spot but without the close up. Annika pursed her lips.

"Yes, I think I know roughly where that is."

"A witness saw a man going into that old church you pointed out. From the description he was dressed for the outdoors. Camo gear and a pack. Could it have been any of your people?"

Annika pursed her lips, eyes glazing for a minute. "Could have been Gareth Bellamy," she finally said.

"No, 'fraid not. I'm looking for someone over six feet and well built."

"Then it's not any of my staff," Annika said definitely.

Mac glanced at the window which was being pelted by rain. He sighed, his clothes already feeling clammy and wet. The jeans had soaked through after his tumble with leaves and mud becoming wedged in his boots, soaking his feet. He wanted to call it a day, stay somewhere warm. Maybe take Hayley up on her offer of a drink and a talk. At that moment, a seat before a fire in a local pub, a glass of the local beer in front of him, sounded like heaven. But duty tugged at his conscience. He had to follow it up.

"We need to make sure this hole is plugged before any of your animals escape," he said. "Regardless of crime scenes or evidence. That has to be the first concern."

"I agree. We can drop some sheep carcasses over on the opposite side of the enclosure. It will draw them away until we can get the fence repaired."

"I need to get a team in there first. Tracker dogs to pick up the scent of blood and forensics. Best would be if you could take the wolves out for the time being."

He was looking at the map; mind full of next steps and at first didn't register the glare that Annika was giving him.

"What are you suggesting? We lock them up in kennels?"

"Yes," Mac said.

"Don't be ridiculous. That would traumatize them."

"Then tranquillise them," Mac suggested.

"And risk them tearing Taz Khan to pieces while he tries to pick off the pack one at a time? Gareth Bellamy is gone, remember? Besides, sedating the animals is a risk to their health."

Kai had wanted Taz charged with assault, pride still hurt at how he'd been hauled off Bellamy. Mac hadn't wanted to be tied up in any more paperwork though. So Taz was still at the park.

"Taz can take you and your team where you need to go while Colin and I monitor the wolves from here. They're all tagged. We can keep in contact with you by radio. If we drop the meat off tonight we can be sure of the pack being where we want them by the early hour's tomorrow morning. If you are ready to go in it will give you the best chance," Annika said.

Mac had to admit it was the most logical plan, though he would just as soon have had the lot of them locked up, trauma or not. He remained silent for a moment, not liking the prospect of going back out there in the dark and, undoubtedly, the rain. Annika must have misinterpreted his silence.

"Mac," she said, quietly.

He looked up in surprise.

"I really would appreciate it if you could meet us halfway on this."

There was the hint of a smile, and her blue eyes looked very big. She was talking more softly than he had heard from her before. It made for an alluring package. Their heads were inches apart and, for one insane moment, Mac wondered what she would do if he leaned in and kissed her.

The idea was in and out of his mind before he could consciously register its presence. He gave her the rogue's grin, and her smile widened a little in return. She was using him, of course. Mac didn't need the greatest empathy to see that.

"Of course, Annika," he said. "Whatever you say,"

## Chapter 14

**M**ac had missed calls from Reid and from Kai. He scrolled through them as he walked to his desk in their makeshift office, wearing clean, dry clothes. Annika had offered him a bedroom at the park, which he'd accepted, staying in the same room he'd been given when he arrived. The rain was loud on the Portakabin's roof, daylight having prematurely fled beneath the thick clouds. The lights were on inside, bright, artificial and headache inducing. Still, at least it was dry. He sat at his desk, seeing a polystyrene cup steaming in the middle of his desk. Lifting his eyes, he gave Melissa a grateful smile, and she winked. Kai and Isla weren't back yet, and he didn't expect to see them anytime soon. Glasgow was five hours' drive away, and he'd ordered Kai and Isla to take hotel rooms at the airport and head up fresh in the morning.

"You eaten yet, Mel?" he asked.

"Soup and a sandwich courtesy of Colin McCauley," she said.

"What time was that?"

"Not long ago. About lunch time."

Mac glanced at his watch. "That was hours ago. Call it a day. There's not much more you can do here, anyway. You staying here at the zoo with me?"

Melissa laughed. "If only, sounds like it'd be fun. I've got a room over a pub in Kingussie."

"Go. That's an order."

Melissa grinned and picked her coat up from the back of her chair.

"I'm waiting on callbacks regarding ownership of Dunachton House. I've spoken to the Land Registry and Companies House as well as all the local estate agents. The place is definitely a front. No individual name coming up, just a lot of nondescript shell companies. I'll chase them up first thing."

She handed him a folder which Mac knew would contain a one-page summary of her work that day, including suggested actions and any hypothesis. Melissa was nothing if not thorough.

"Thanks, Mel. See you tomorrow."

"If you want to swing by the Royal Oak for a drink and a bite to eat later, I think Hayley said she'd taken a room there too," Melissa said with a mischievous grin.

"What goes on in Kingussie stays in Kingussie," Mac replied. "I won't tell your wife."

Melissa stuck her tongue out at him. "She's been asking a lot of questions about you, sir. That's all I'm saying. Good night."

Mac stared into space as the door closed behind Melissa. He had to follow up with Kai and with Reid, but part of him wanted to grab his coat and follow his DI to the village. The Royal Oak was probably quiet, with a roaring fire and a good guest ale. And Hayley had been asking about him? A smile ghosted across his face until he became aware of it. This wasn't the time. He reached for his phone, scrolling to Annika's number, and called her.

"Annika, Mac, still in the office?"

"Yes, you?"

"I'll be working for a while yet. Would you be free to take me up to that old church? I'd like to get a look up there."

"Now?"

"Yes. There won't be time later. It's probably got no bearing on the case, but I won't know until I've been there and I probably won't find it by myself."

He hoped the suggestion of helpless male need appealed to some kind of nurturing instinct in Annika. Or maybe just professional pride at how well she knew her own project. The roads leading to the church weren't exactly well marked on maps anymore and Mac doubted that vorsprung durch technik would be a match for the roads around here.

"Sure," Annika said with a slight sigh. "Actually it'll be good to get out for a bit. I've been cooped up all day. Meet me in the car park. We'll need to go now if you want to see it in daylight."

She was waiting by a muddy Land Rover when Mac. She'd let her hair down and it fell to her shoulders in white gold waves. Somehow, it did little to soften her looks. Simply added a touch of savage wildness. As he approached, she swept it back with the fingers of one hand and covered it with a baseball cap. She drove them away from the park and onto the A9, heading south towards Kingussie. Before reaching it, she turned off onto a side-road that Mac hadn't even spotted until they were turning into it. It was barely large enough to accommodate the Land Rover and seemed to get tighter as they wove between tall hedgerows.

"So, are you any closer to finding the owner of the finger?" Annika asked.

"Are we causing you some inconvenience?" Mac asked.

"Of course," Annika replied with Scandinavian directness.

"I know who it belonged to and now that we know where they entered the enclosure, I'm hoping we'll find out more. As to who did it?" he shrugged.

"So it was murder then?"

"Aye, looks like it," Mac replied.

Rain was starting to hit the windscreen. Back in the woods, following the tracker dogs, he'd been able to ignore the rain and the anxiety it brought on. Sitting as a passenger in a car, there was nothing to occupy his mind. He felt a tightness in his chest and a sudden clamminess to his skin. Annika had glanced at him, then did a double take.

"Are you OK? You don't get car sick do you?"

"No," Mac replied tightly. "I'm fine."

"You don't look it. You're white as a sheet. Seriously, this car is a mess but I don't want to stink it out with vomit."

A passing place appeared, and she swung the Land Rover into it, coming to a halt.

"I'm not going to be sick, ok?" Mac said. "It's nothing. Let's get on with it."

Annika shrugged. "I'm first aid trained and I have some medical knowledge. You don't look well."

"It's just…" Mac considered his words, wanting the questions to stop. "I get…a bit anxious at times."

Annika pulled out onto the road. "When you're in a car?" she asked, driving on.

Mac sighed through gritted teeth, seeking the inner peace of grounding himself in the moment. The smell of the old land rover's interior, wet mud, and damp clothes.

The sound of the rain on the windscreen. The beautiful woman sitting a foot away from him.

"No, the rain brings it on," he confessed, feeling as though he had pulled a tooth.

"Ah, physiological reaction to certain stimulus that triggers a traumatic memory," Annika said, nodding sagely.

Mac's head whipped around. "You have a degree in psychology too?" he said, somewhat incredulous.

"Of course not. My doctorate is strictly zoological. My mother is a successful psychiatrist in Stockholm though."

"Wonderful," Mac breathed.

"It's not uncommon. I have a similar trigger relating to large bodies of water. I almost drowned in a fjord when I was seven. Large lakes, rivers, ocean. Brings me out in a cold sweat. I hate the beach. It's nothing to be ashamed of."

"Who says I'm ashamed?" Mac shot back.

"Your defensive attitude. I don't think any the less of you. I'm sure you're just as good at your job as I am at mine. What was it?"

Mac laughed at a sudden sense of absurdity. Annika was so blunt it was almost as though she couldn't comprehend how direct and inappropriate her questions were. The thought occurred whether she was also on the spectrum. It was a concept Clio had suggested to him about himself and had made sense of a lot of character traits he'd always regarded as weaknesses. Like being uncomfortable in social settings, the inability to read and interpret subtle emotional clues in a person's face, or interacting with his team on anything but a professional level.

"Take your pick. I had a childhood from hell. Mother died before I really knew her. Brother ran off to join the navy, haven't seen him for years. Sister murdered and dad topped himself," Mac said in a rush.

"At least you can say it. That's progress. Bet you couldn't even think about it at one point," Annika said.

Mac felt an easing in his chest; breathing was coming easier even though the rain was pounding harder. He ran a hand through his hair, still damp from the soaking earlier. Annika was disturbingly perceptive.

"You're right. I'm in therapy and I have a good friend who's helped me a lot," he admitted.

Annika nodded. "I've been in therapy for years. Comes from having a father who was prominent in his field, a field I subsequently chose. He studied law while writing his doctoral thesis on a new species of insect he'd discovered and then went into politics. To cap it all, it was thanks to his influence in the European Commission I got the funding for the rewilding project."

"Talk about daddy issues," Mac said drily.

Annika laughed. It was deep and musical, a complete contrast to the tough, glacial exterior she liked to project.

"Think yourself lucky your dad topped himself. Nothing worse than competing with a parent who won't stop achieving."

Mac shook his head, chuckling. "No-one's ever told me to be thankful my dad ate rat poison and blew his head off with a shotgun. That's dark, Annika."

She shrugged. "I'm a Swede. This is it up ahead."

She pointed to where a dark, square stone shape had appeared, alone in a field off to one side. Annika pulled in front of a mouldering wooden gate, nudging it with the Land Rover to push it open. She stopped just inside. The church was missing its steeple, which ended raggedly just above the roofline. That roof was missing for half its length, revealing exposed beams. No glass occupied any of the windows. Against the dark sky and framed by driving rain, it looked forlorn.

"Wow! I've not been up here since I started the project. Look at that. Looks like a black metal album cover," Annika breathed.

She took out her phone and snapped a picture.

"You a metal head?" Mac asked with interest.

Annika looked at him and said with a deadpan expression. "I'm a Swede."

"Me too. The metal I mean," Mac replied. "Who do you listen to?"

"A lot of Norwegian bands from the old days. Darkthrone, Mayhem, Burzum. That kind of thing. Of course, Abba is my all-time favourite,"

Mac laughed as he opened the door. "Aye, you're a Swede, eh?"

Hands deep in his pockets, he strode towards the church. The rain lashed his face and ran into the raised collar of his jacket, but he refused to hunch his shoulders or drop his face. Rain was a fact of life in Scotland, particularly in the highlands. Even more so on Skye. He wasn't about to cringe away from weather. Annika strode alongside, long-legged and with head also raised. He felt a companionable bond with her, a thawing in the ice between them, and wondered if she felt it too? Hayley flashed briefly into his mind, but her pretty eyes and blushing face didn't compare to Annika's cruel beauty and brutal honesty. Valkyrie was right. Close up, he could see the entrance to the church had, at one time, been boarded up. A fence had been erected around it, bearing the name of a contractor. The concrete blocks securing the wire-links hadn't been a match for the wind and it had toppled against the church or lay flat on the ground. The boards over the door wouldn't be so vulnerable, but several lay on the ground in front of the arched stone doorway. Mac crouched and produced a pen torch from his pocket. The doors looked to have rotted at the bottom, and the missing boards now exposed a hole directly into the building.

He sighed and put the torch into his mouth before getting onto hands and knees and crawling through the hole. On the other side was icy stone, wet with rain and mud. He heard Annika following him.

"Don't. Stay where you are."

"Yeah, OK," Annika said as she crawled through.

Mac straightened and shone the torch around. They were in some kind of porch area that ended in another set of doors. They were unlocked. Beyond was the church itself. No pews remained, just a row of squat columns supporting a vaulted roof until the roof disappeared and daylight flooded in along with the rain. The air smelled of cold stone and fetid mud. Something clattered under Mac's boot. Looking down, he saw an empty can. Hot dog sausages, eat hot or cold. Against the wall were two empty tins of baked beans next to some rectangular foil packets. Taking a pair of gloves from a pocket, he picked up the hot dog tin. The use by date was a good eighteen months into the future. This hadn't been left here years before. It had been bought and consumed this year.

"Has there been a tramp here?" Annika asked.

"Seems a long way for a tramp to come with a heavy bag full of tins," Mac said, shaking his head. "I expect to find rough sleepers in derelict buildings in the city, where they'll be close to food or drugs. Whatever they need. Not out in the middle of nowhere."

He straightened and walked to the silver packet. A crumbly powder clung to the insides.

"They look like MREs," Annika said.

"What?"

"Meals Ready to Eat. The military use them for soldiers. Dehydrated and concentrated, high calorie. I've used them when I was tracking a wolf pack through the Canadian Rockies. "

Mac thought of the description that Smilley had given him. A big man in camo gear, carrying a large backpack. Was he looking for an ex-squaddie? He shone the torch around the area where the food debris seemed to be concentrated. It fell onto something white at the bottom of the wall. The stone had been scored away down near the floor, scratched by something sharp. An inscription had been carved into the stone. LW 17/11/01. He frowned. On its own, he would have put it down as a signature with date marking when the person had been there. But the food tins certainly didn't date from 2001. They could have been left by two separate people, but instinct told Mac this wasn't the case. Someone had been here for a while, long enough to eat a few meals. And while they'd sat here, they'd passed the time by carving their initials and a date. He took out his phone and snapped several pictures of the carving and the tins. It took an hour to search the rest of the building, but there was no sign its visitor had strayed beyond the area closest to the entrance.

A hypothesis was forming in his mind. A man came here to hide. Ex-army and ready to camp out, comfortable living outdoors. He has something sharp enough to mark the ancient stone of the church. And to cut bullets out of bodies and walls. He goes over to Dunachton House and kills three people. One person is removed from the house and left for the wolves. He doesn't return to his hideout. Where was he now? Why had he done it? To complete a contract?

# Chapter 15

"Thanks, Annika," Mac said as they arrived back at the park.

"I can't say no to a policeman, can I?" Annika replied. "I would like to get back to my work as soon as possible and to avoid any of this getting into the press. Anything I can do to help that happen, I must do."

"On that subject. Do you know a local journalist called Neill Smilley?"

Annika frowned, switching off the engine. "There was a reporter from a local rag asking for interviews a while ago. I don't remember his name."

"Well, he's got it in for your project. That's why he's sniffing around. I may have bought you a bit of breathing space. Put the fear of god in him, but in my experience, the press doesn't stay quiet forever. I need to get a forensics team up to that church, as well as check out the area around the breach in your enclosure. We're going to be around for a while yet."

Maybe that wouldn't be so bad, he thought, watching Annika for a reaction. She took off her hat, running her hand through her silvery-gold hair and her icy blue eyes pinned him.

"Yes, well, we'll just have to make the best of it. Are you done for the day, Detective Chief Inspector?"

"Mac."

"Mac," Annika repeated then clamped the hat back onto her head and pulled the brim down to shade her eyes.

Mac glanced at his watch.

"I have a few calls to make first. How about you?"

"A mountain of work to catch up on. But I'll see you in a few hours before you head out with Taz." Annika said abruptly.

Rogue's grin. Shut down just as he was thinking he was getting somewhere. Mac got out of the car and walked to the mobile HQ, unlocking it with a key from an inside pocket. He heard the Land Rover driving on towards the park's staff parking. He flicked on the overhead lights and walked to his desk, taking out his phone and skimming the messages. Sitting down he tossed his wet jacket over the nearest chair and put his feet up on the desk, dialling Kai.

"Guv."

"Sorry, I couldn't get back to you before now. How did you get on?" Mac said.

"We identified our two victims. Sofia Ivanova and Katya Bilyk. Saw them coming through immigration and got their visa applications pulled up by passport control. They came to the UK on refugee visas with a UK sponsor and address. We checked out the sponsor. A couple called Bartosz. Mr. and Mrs. They have an address in the Inch. I called the number given, pretended to be calling from the Home

Office, checking up. I spoke to someone who gave his name as Matusz Bartosz, which matches the visa documentation. He lied to my face. Told me that Sofia and Katya had settled in well and were very happy in their new home. They were both out sightseeing, apparently," Kai chuckled. "Gotcha."

"What did you say?" Mac asked.

"Jolly good," Kai put on an English accent. "Glad to hear it, old chap. I'll speak to them soon. Got off the phone before he could ask me any questions."

"Good work. Send me over the address, and I'll go and speak to Mr. and Mrs. Bartosz."

"Isla looked them up. They run a Polish deli, lot of cash going in and out. She's checked in with her team but the Bartosz's aren't on anyone's radar."

"What about the two women's movements after the airport. Were they met?"

"Yes. A blonde woman. Matches the pictures we got from CCTV locally. We got her passport application from border control, too. Everything ties up. The woman in the pictures is Isabella North, and she left the airport with them. I would need to get back onto the mainframe to log into the motorway cameras to trace where they went from the airport, though."

"We know where they ended up but it would be good to know the route they took. Get back to Edinburgh tomorrow and get to work on that. Good work both of you."

"No bother, guv. Isla's been a real asset. Wish she wasn't working for the dark side."

"Does she think Musa is going to want our case?" Mac asked, suddenly alert.

Kai's voice dropped a notch, as though Isla was in the room. "Aye, she does. It's looking like those two women were trafficked into the country. They end up dead along with their courier."

"Has she spoken to him?"

"Not yet. I've charmed her," Kai said.

Mac hung up, putting the phone down and staring into space for a moment. Any investigation was time sensitive. DNA evidence could be lost, especially when it was exposed to the elements. Witnesses' memories of an event could change in a matter of hours, let alone days or weeks. And the longer it went on, the more chance of a cleanup operation being mounted. Especially if the evidence led to an organisation like Allen's or Lowe's. But now they knew that Sofia and Katya had been trafficked and they had a weak link in the chain. Two people prepared to be a front for a phony visa application. From them, Mac could break the chain, get into the operation, and find its head. The phone lit up, and he saw Kenny Reid's name appear. He picked it up again.

"Sir," he answered.

A slurp and a gulp. Reid was having a wee dram. He wasn't the type to stay hydrated, and it was now after seven. So, more than likely whisky.

"Mac. What have you got for me?"

Mac took a deep breath, ready for the explosion. "Sorry, guv, but this is looking more and more like a turf war. I've identified the two victims; they've been trafficked here for prostitution. I'm going to see the people who vouched for them on their visa applications. But, Dunachton House was a classic hit. I've got evidence that it was planned well in advance by a professional prepared to camp out in the area waiting for his opportunity. He was methodical and professional, even taking the time to remove bullets from the scene and bodies so that his weapon couldn't be traced. I'd put money on this being a move by Hance Allen against his chief rival."

Reid swore. "Allen's no good to me, Mac. I need Lowe taken down."

"I know that, sir. I'm just telling you how the evidence is going."

"Right, well you're going to have to show a bit more imagination, son," Reid snapped. "I've been talking to a couple of my old snouts. One of them is Mary Fraser; she's a tom working in Edinburgh. I've been paying her for information for years. She gave me a couple of names of younger girls being run by John Lowe. Or rather by his girl-friend, an American who sounds just like our missing person. They didn't exactly have a smooth relationship, you know? The gossip is that they had a massive falling out and Isabella ran to get away from John. Look into that angle, Mac, will you?"

"Ok, give me the names."

Mac picked up a pen and scribbled down two names and noted what patch they worked. It was worth a look. If John Lowe had wanted rid of his fiancée it wouldn't be beyond him to make it look like an attack on himself.

"It's not implausible, right?" Reid said, slurping again.

"Not implausible, sir. There's an angle there."

"Good. I've got Lowe breathing down my neck, wanting a result. Jesus, I cannae believe I'm being leaned on by a crook and not some eejit of a boss. Get me out of this, Mac."

"We're tracing the last movements of Isabella North and the two women she was trafficking. I've got a lead in Edinburgh, a couple who were named as sponsors on the two women's visas. They look like stooges. It could give us an in on Lowe's organisation if we put the pressure on them. Kai is going to trace Isabella's movements from the airport where she was last seen."

"Just find me something that links her disappearance to John Lowe. That's all I want, Mac," Reid said, cutting him off.

There was a belligerence in his voice that made Mac think he had imbibed more than one before he'd picked up the phone. There was a ragged edge to Reid that Mac hadn't seen before. He was feeling the pressure. For him to be exhibiting as much as he was, the pressure must be intense.

"Then keep Musa off my back and out of my patch," Mac shot back, matching steel for steel.

Reid sighed. "I'll do what I can."

The call was over. Mac was left feeling tired and beaten. The case was nowhere near over. As time went on, pieces became visible, but the overall picture was still a mystery. There was a man out there without a conscience, capable of killing brutally and without hesitation. He was a careful planner, capable of putting himself in discomfort to wait out his prey. A real psycho. Men like that didn't come around all that often. Mac's instinct was that this was the ultimate professional, which meant someone was paying him. But who? He ran his fingers through his hair, looking through the forensics reports Hayley had put together, looking for anything in the evidence gathered that would give him the insight he needed. He glanced at his watch. Thoughts went to the Royal Oak in Kingussie. He wondered if Hayley was having dinner with Melissa. Maybe having a drink to decompress. His eyes went back to the screen. It went blank as he touched the power button and got up, grabbing his jacket. As he left the mobile HQ, he looked towards the more permanent temporary buildings which housed Annika and her team.

Most of the windows were dark, but a few were lit. He tried to map the geography of those buildings in his head, tried to figure out if one of those windows looked in on Annika's office. Wondered how she would react if he knocked on her door. Mac turned away from the light and walked towards his car. She would tell him she was busy and send him on his way with a few well-chosen words and the careful use of his police rank. The rain had abated, but the ground was soggy. He splashed through the mud to his car and got in. Ten minutes later, he was pulling into the car park of the Royal Oak. Inside was a quiet country pub. There were half a dozen patrons at most, and the only sound was the dull murmur of conversation and the occasional sonic burp of the fruit machine. The main bar was dim, lit by a wood fire, crackling merrily in a blackened stone fireplace. Mismatched sofa and armchairs were positioned around the fire along with a coffee table on which were placed a selection of paperbacks and a dominos set.

Hayley sat in a tall, wing-backed armchair, holding a glass of wine, and reading a book. There was no sign of Melissa. Mac approached and Hayley's eyes went above the rim of her glass as she sipped from it. They met Mac's. As the glass was lowered she bit her lip and the corners of her mouth tugged into a smile.

"Glad you could make it," she said.

"Melissa not staying up to keep you company?" Mac asked.

"No, she wanted to call home and then get an early night. I thought I would hang on here, on the off chance."

Mac sat in a chair next to hers. "On the off chance of what?"

Hayley raised an eyebrow. "That you might be along. Melissa doubted it. She said you would be too buried in the case."

"There's only so much I can do right now. I have some leads to follow back in Edinburgh. And I want to see if we can find any more trace of Isabella North. To do both I have to wait."

Hayley put the book down on the table and sat back again, both hands around her glass. The firelight sparkled in her eyes in quite an alluring way. Mac enjoyed watching it. She seemed to enjoy being watched, showing no signs of discomfort as Mac held eye contact long enough that neither could be in doubt.

"Any closer to finding the person who did this?" Hayley asked.

"Maybe. We found where he camped out while he waited for his victims. I think he might be ex-military."

Hayley's eyebrows went up. "That's a breakthrough."

Mac shrugged. "Doesn't bring me any closer to catching him. I also now know that the date 17th November 2001 is significant and the letters LW."

Hayley looked away long enough to put down her wine-glass. She cleared her throat. "Where did that come up?"

"Scratched into a wall at a disused church. With something sharp. Almost like he was passing the time. Who knows what it means. Some significant event, birth, death, anniversary…could be anything."

Hayley smiled again. "And the letters?"

"Initials? No way to tell. Just have to hope that we get closer and it takes on some meaning for us," Mac said.

He was beginning to think that the evening would be spent talking about the case. Hayley suddenly seemed very interested, and he remembered how she had, apparently, requested the case and professed her admiration of some of his previous investigations. Was Hayley just a murder nerd? She might also have been a mind reader.

"Are we going to sit here talking shop all night?" she asked a playful smile on her face.

"Hell, no," Mac replied. Rogue's grin.

## Chapter 16

"**H**ey! You're going to be late!"

Mac woke with a start, blinking at the black beams of the low-ceilinged room. There was a moment of disorientation as he fought to remember where he was. Then a pillow hit him in the face. Hayley was half dressed, the top half in a t-shirt baggy enough to hide her shape. She also wore thick socks, but nothing else below the waist. Half-naked was somehow more enticing that fully. Mac rolled to his front in the bed, realizing that he was naked and running hands over his face. His shoulders were sore and his eyes were grainy, as though he had awakened from a deep sleep after getting far too little. That had actually been the case, he recalled.

"Late?"

"You said that Annika Eklund and her team would be putting down meat to lure the wolves? So we can get into the enclosure?" Hayley grinned, tying back unruly hair.

Reality slammed home into Mac's mind. He had a vague memory of a dream about Clio. It had left him with a disturbing sense of guilt. As though he had just been unfaithful. It was a ridiculous thought. Clio was a good friend, but there had never been any suggestion of romance. Or even just plain old sex. They had been colleagues on a case, Clio acting as an expert consultant. Then they'd been survivors of the same trauma and become good friends because of the shared experience. Mac sat up as Hayley threw him his jeans, t-shirt, and jumper. She seemed full of life and smiles. He felt full of gravel and mud.

"Can you pass me those jeans?" she asked, pointing to his side of the bed.

Mac looked and saw her jeans on the floor. He picked them up as she took a pair of panties from a suitcase. As he picked up the jeans, he felt something in the pocket. Something small, rectangular, and hard. His eyes went to Hayley, who was looking over her shoulder at him as she pulled on her underwear. He shot her the rogue's grin, letting his gaze rest on her backside. She smiled and blushed. Mac felt a sense of warmth at that smile, a comfortable contentment. Thoughts of what Hayley kept in her jeans pockets retreated to the back of his mind, but did not disappear entirely. He was remembering a sudden moment of clumsiness in the back of a car and a missing SD card. Shit.

"I need the loo," Hayley announced with what would have been charming, innocent candour under other circumstances. "Unless you need the bathroom?"

"I'm good," Mac said.

He put his hand in the pocket as the bathroom door closed and pulled out the SD card. If he put it back, there was a risk she would dispose of it. If he kept it, she might miss it and realise he had it. Mac knew he should call in Melissa as a witness and make this formal. Hayley was sabotaging the case, removing evidence. The only reason he could think of was because she knew the killer. She was working to protect his identity. Which meant that any DNA evidence gathered was suspect. On the other hand, letting her believe she was undetected would be an opportunity to potentially track the killer through her. The toilet was flushing, taps running. Mac knew he had seconds to decide. As the bathroom door opened, he dropped the SD card to the floor atop his own jeans and threw back the sheets. Hayley froze in the bathroom door as Mac got out of bed naked and walked towards her, jeans in hands. She bit her lip hard enough to make it white. Mac remembered the touch of those even white teeth.

He knelt in front of her, offering to dress her in the jeans, and she giggled. Mac made the act of pulling the garment up her legs into a long, drawn-out process with a lot of kissing and touching that made Hayley rise on her toes as he pulled up the zip, face level with her midriff.

"We don't have time for this, you tease," she whispered.

"No," Mac said, grinning a smoky, smouldering smile as he stood. "Maybe later."

Hayley grabbed him for a long kiss. Mac eventually extricated himself and went to dress, conscious of her eyes on him. He had partitioned his mind, one half seeing her as a suspect to be watched, the other revelling in the sexual chemistry between them. The SD card was palmed as he dressed and then stowed in a back pocket. Hayley didn't seem to have missed it. After using the bathroom, he followed her out of the room and down the stairs to the pub's back door and night-time entrance for guests. Mac's vehicle was parked in the car park behind the pub. Hayley went to her own; Mac considered asking her to travel with him, but dismissed the idea. She might think it the act of a lover wanting to keep her close for a few more minutes. Or she might suss that he wanted to keep his eye on her. He knew where she was going, anyway. In the car he cranked up the radio, if only for a few minutes, drowning out the voice of his conscience with raw, furious Norwegian metal. Misanthropy and distorted guitars assaulted him and washed through him like a black tide.

A child born in 2001 would be twenty-three by now. The idea popped into his head without warning. Lisa. Laura. Louise. L could be a lot of names and that was just the female ones. No reason it couldn't be a man's name. The idea occurred to Mac that the inscription in the church had reminded him of those men and women who had their children's initials and dates of birth tattooed on their body. It was done as a demonstration to the world of their devotion. A way to remember and commemorate a lost child. This had been done where no-one was likely to see it for years. If ever. Not a proclamation to the world. A very private message then. For one person and one god? He didn't know why his mind was working this way suddenly. Maybe it was the anti-Christian lyrical theme of the music. Maybe it was something in the dream he couldn't remember. Or just the onslaught of endorphins from a night with Hayley. A man memorialising his child before embarking on a murder spree. Why?

He pulled into the wildlife park, and the gates were unlocked and opened. Hayley's headlights appeared around a bend behind him. He pulled in; fascinated by the twists and turns his brain was taking. Why make that inscription? What did it signify? A wife long lost? A child dead? Or just lost to an estranged father? Was it a symbol of regret or of a promise made? He shook his head. All these ideas could be nonsense or one of those notions could be spot on. No way of knowing, but if he sat there all night, he thought he might spend the entire time coming up with different explanations. It was linked, though. Of that, every instinct he had was screaming at him. He waited for Hayley to pull up next to him and got out. She smiled cheekily as she caught his eye, and Mac gave her a wink. They walked towards the lighted windows of one of the pre-fab buildings. Dawn was staining the far sky, making the sky pale while it remained dark and starry in the opposite direction.

"Thank you for staying with me," Hayley whispered, looking around hastily.

Mac nodded. "Sorry, to get all unprofessional," he said.

"That's OK. I thought you might not be there when I woke up. I wouldn't have had a problem with that," Hayley said, adding the last hurriedly.

Mac wanted to ask her why. Tell her she should have a problem with it. Tell her to run a mile from him because his head was a mess and two other women were vying for space at the front of it. Clio was there despite the absence of any hint of romance between them. Or even just plain old lust. Annika was there too. A dangerous siren. Fierce and independent.

"I wouldn't do that to you," Mac said.

That got a smile. It had been true but Mac hadn't intended it to sound as loaded with meaning as it had. He ran a hand through his hair, waving Hayley ahead of him into the building. Taz looked out of the staff room. He was kitted out for a hike and had a rifle shaped bag slung over his shoulder. A couple of Hayley's forensics' team were also present along with Colin McCauley.

"Ready for your adventure, Detective Chief Inspector?" he said, brightly.

"As I'll ever be. Everything OK your end?"

"Aye. The wolves took some persuading right enough.

149

They were clustering at a spot not far from the breach in the fence. I don't think they'd found it yet. We've not got a camera in that section, but their trackers showed them in and around a small copse of trees about a mile from the gap. We had to put in quite a lot of fresh meat to tempt them away, but they're on the move now. By the time you get to the gap, they'll be three miles away. Which they can run in about half an hour, so don't hang about," he grinned.

———

ONCE AGAIN, the mountain rescue dogs had the scent. They were followed by their handlers and then Taz through the same thick woodland that Mac had fought his way through previously. They crossed streams of icy water and clambered earth banks of leaf mulch and mud. A mile, McCauley had said. Mac felt as though he'd been walking for ten. But they finally reached a thick copse at the bottom of a dell within the boundaries of the wolf enclosure. Taz descended the slope in a series of angled steps and slides, gun held with the casual readiness of an expert. Mac was glad of it. It had occurred to him he was relying, potentially for his life, on a man whose best friend had been arrested by Mac and was probably going down for a few years. He didn't know how close Bellamy and Taz had actually been, however, and he hoped it was a casual laddish acquaintanceship with minimal loyalty. Now would be the perfect time for some vindictive revenge. Hayley was ahead of him, coping with the landscape and the pace with apparent ease. Her team, each carrying rucksacks full of gear they would need to examine any potential crime scene, were behind Mac, keeping close. Taz was speaking into a radio and then turning to wave towards a spot off to their left. Mac looked and eventually saw the CCTV camera, secured to a tree trunk a few yards away.

"The trail ends up in that copse," Taz said to Mac with a head nod in the relevant direction.

Mac was pleased to see the younger man was breathing hard. Glad he wasn't the only one who'd found the pace difficult. He really needed to think seriously about his fitness levels if these were the sort of cases he'd be investigating. The handlers moved forward at a walk, towards the trees, but before they could enter the copse, the dogs were on their hind legs, pawing at the air in front of them, eyes drawn upward.

"This is the spot the wolves were concentrated on too," Taz said.

Mac was looking at the area the dogs had fixated on. At first, nothing was obvious in the pale morning light. Then he saw a bag hanging from an upper branch of one of the trees. It stood out against the skeletal bare fingers of the tree, which seemed to claw at the naked sky. Taz followed his eyes along with everyone else's.

"Oh, my god. What the hell is that?" he breathed in a voice alive with dread.

"How do we get it down?" Hayley asked.

"There's a ladder against the tree," Cameron pointed, kneeling beside his dog to reward its efforts with a treat. "You should be able to get to the branch below it and reach from there."

Mac went forward. The ladder looked to be lightweight but of metal, the kind that folded up to a manageable carrying size. It led to a bough about twelve feet off the ground which rose upward at a steep angle to within reach of the bag tied to the branch above. Steep but manageable.

Whoever had tied the bag up there had left the means to recover it. Which meant they wanted it found. Mac put on a pair of latex gloves and tested the first rungs of the ladder.

"I should go first," Hayley said. "I'm lighter than you."

Mac looked from her to the flimsy-looking ladder, but then shook his head. There was no way he was letting her near potential evidence first.

"If the man who put that bag up there is the man Smilley saw, he's not little. If he could get up there, then so can I," Mac said, hoping he was coming across as gallant rather than suspicious.

He looked across to the mountain rescue team. "Either of you got a knife?" he asked.

Jake offered a penknife. He unfolded the blade, showing it to Mac, and then folded it back, making it safe.

"Maybe carry it in your mouth. You might not be able to spare a hand once you get up there to take it out of your pocket," he suggested. "Maybe Cam or I should go up?"

Mac shook his head again. He felt like he was being led by the nose. The killer had left a hole in the fence, knowing it would eventually be found. Then a trail of blood to follow. Now, something the dogs could smell was hanging from a tree. It was a tableau. A presentation. He had dealt with enough serial killers, intent on making their crimes into works of art, to recognise it. It made him determined to be the one to go up.

"If you fall and break a leg I don't want you suing Police Scotland, eh? They insure me for this," Mac joked before clamping the knife between his teeth.

He climbed the ladder, hearing it creak ominously beneath his weight but holding. The last couple of rungs he grabbed the bough it led to and hauled himself up. After a moment of swinging his legs in space, he got his body up onto the branch with legs dangling to either side. Using the trunk, he stood, wavering, and almost falling, but managed by sheer force of will and tenacity to avoid that humiliation. Feeling as though he was walking a tightrope, he edged along the branch, hands in front of him as the angle steepened. The bark was rough enough that there was plenty of grip and eventually he half-stood, half-crouched below the bag. Hayley had removed her coat and was holding one side of it like a safety net beneath him, one of her team holding the other.

"You can let it drop," she said. "Just cut the rope and we'll catch it."

"Easier said than done," Mac muttered.

"You'll have to jump," Cameron suggested. "Just a couple of feet up would do it, grab the bottom of the bag and then swipe with the knife. It's sharp enough."

Mac was peering up and saw that the cord holding the bag wasn't very thick. It didn't look like he would need to saw through it. One swipe might indeed do it. He edged higher up the branch and saw the inscription that had been carved into the wood, just above where one of his hands rested. Four vertical lines next to each other. Risking his precarious balance and almost losing it, he fumbled his phone from the pocket of his coat and managed to balance long enough to snap a picture. Then a gust of wind hit him and his arms were wind milling. The phone fell. Mac would have joined it, but at the last minute, he jumped. Knife still clenched in his teeth, he grabbed for the nearest handhold, which happened to be the bag. For a moment, all of his weight hung on it and then the line holding it snapped. Mac dropped the bag as he fell, briefly caught the branch he'd been standing on, but it caught him under his chin. He bit his tongue, and the pain made him lose his grip. He landed on his back at the foot of the tree, air rushing from him.

Mac spat blood, rolled slowly onto his side and sucked in a ragged breath. Cameron knelt beside him.

"You, OK?" he asked.

Mac nodded. "Don't think I broke anything except my pride," he finally said, spitting out more blood from his bleeding tongue.

He looked towards Hayley, who knelt beside the makeshift net she had used to catch the bag. She was untying a drawstring and opening the bag, pulling the material down to reveal what was inside. Mac gingerly got to his feet and staggered over, looking down as Hayley sat back, mouth open. Someone retched loudly, coughing and choking. Mac stared down at the severed head. It was a woman with long blonde hair. Bullet hole above the left eyebrow. The eyes had been removed and the letters LW had been carved into the forehead.

# Chapter 17

Mac called Melissa as he drove back to the mobile HQ. The bag with its grisly contents sat in the passenger footwell of his car. He'd insisted on keeping custody of it until it was back in the mobile lab facilities. Hayley had looked confused but had accepted his decision.

"Mel, just wanted to check you were in the office," Mac said as his DI answered.

"I'm here, guv."

"Good, I'm bringing in Isabella North's head. Don't ask me, I don't have time. It's going on ice until Derek Stringer can look at it. No matter what it takes I want him up here to review all of Hayley's findings. I'll go to Reid or to the DCC if I need to."

"Do you have a reason to doubt Hayley's findings?" Mel asked.

"She concealed evidence. I found the SD card from Neill Smilley's camera in her jeans. She must have taken it after dropping the camera. The only reason I can think of is she knows who the killer is and is working to conceal his identity."

"You found it in her jeans? You searched her?" Mel asked.

"She wasn't wearing them at the time," Mac said, irritable at having to discuss his personal life and at himself for blurring the professional and personal lines in the first place.

"I understand," Mel said, voice devoid of any kind of judgement.

Mac gave an exasperated growl. "I didn't find the SD card until this morning. I had no reason to suspect her before I slept with her, ok? There's no conflict of interest here."

"No, guv."

Mac swore. His annoyance was directed purely at himself, not at Melissa's reaction. He'd given in to weakness, flattered by Hayley's attention and wound up with the chemistry he felt with Annika Eklund.

"Sorry, Mel. That wasn't aimed at you. I'm kicking myself."

"Don't, guv. You've done nothing wrong. Ill-advised perhaps, but not wrong."

"We document everything. I won't risk losing the case for a one-night stand. I'll prepare a statement and you can file it with the case notes."

He was pulling into the car park now. Hayley's car was right behind him.

"I'm coming in now. I'll bring Hayley into the office and you can read her rights to her. We'll record the interview. By the book."

Mac thought he could hear the smile in Mel's voice as she replied, perhaps even with a touch of relief. "Yes, guv."

Leaning over, Mac grabbed the bag by the strings that

secured it. It was a duffel-type bag made of a synthetic material that appeared to be waterproof. No blood had leaked though, it had pooled in the bottom. The smell must have drawn the wolves, though, with only the scent of fresher meat drawing them away. Taz Khan had remained with two members of Hayley's forensics team who were documenting the scene. Annika and Colin were monitoring the wolves and would provide plenty of warning if the animals decided to return. Cameron and Jake had been recruited into making makeshift repairs to the fence using any materials they could lay their hands on. Once everyone had finally exited the enclosure, they would do their best to close up the gap temporarily until Annika could get a contractor to do a more permanent job. At least there wouldn't be a public health emergency added to Mac's plate. Hayley was getting out of her car, and Mac jerked his head towards the main office of the mobile HQ.

"Shouldn't we get that on ice in the lab?" she asked.

"Come in here first," Mac replied, walking to the door, and opening it for her.

Hayley followed more slowly. As she did, Mac watched her put her hands into the pockets of her jeans. Her step faltered. Mac's eyes never left her and when she looked back at him he saw the idea of flight crossing her mind.

"Don't do it, Hayley," he said, gently. "Step inside and we'll talk."

Her chin lifted, and an expression came over her face he hadn't seen before. It was determined and hard. Not a repentant face. Finally, she nodded and preceded Mac into the office. Mel was waiting and Mac closed the door behind him as she began reading Hayley her rights.

"Take a seat," Mac said, pushing a wheeled chair

towards her. He sat on a desk in front of her. Mel took up a position to one side, phone set to record.

Mac produced the SD card from his pocket.

"Obviously, my prints are on this now. We'll find yours too as well as Neill Smilley's," he said. "And his pictures. He'll identify it for us. So that just leaves the question of why you took it?"

"I found it on the floor of your car after I dropped the camera," Hayley said.

"I know. I asked why you took it," Mac replied.

"I didn't know I had. I picked it up and thought it was mine," Hayley replied with confidence.

"Yours? You carry around SD cards for digital cameras?" Mac asked.

"I carry all sorts of things," Hayley said. "And I'm always losing them. It's embarrassing. I haven't lost something that's been found by a member of the public, thank god. And not something that's been material evidence on a case. But, I'm always losing things. You saw how chaotic my room at the hotel was. Panties in one corner. Jeans in another…"

She bit her lip and casually glanced towards Mel.

"For the tape, I had sexual relations with Hayley Blackwood on the night of…" Mac reeled of the date and the approximate time. "I discovered the SD card in her jeans pocket while we were dressing the following morning."

Hayley's smile slipped. Her story had been plausible. Field pathologists carried and used digital cameras. Hayley's work bag was probably full of memory sticks, SD cards, cables, as well as other accessories of a forensic investigator. It was her reaction. When she realised the SD card was no longer in her pocket. When she realised she was being cautioned. She'd probably prided herself on not giving in to panic. But panic was a natural reaction for an innocent person being cautioned by the police. Only guilty people took it in their stride. They knew nothing could be given away from this point on. Knew they had to hold their nerve and wait for the police to show their cards.

"Tell me why you took the SD card from Neill Smilley's camera," Mac said.

"I didn't," Hayley replied.

"Were you in it with him? Did he offer you money to keep the card safe until he could publish the pictures?" Mac persisted.

"I didn't take it," Hayley said, not looking at him.

"Or was it to conceal the identity of the man in those pictures," Mac asked.

His tongue was throbbing and there was an ache in the small of his back where a stone or a root had jabbed him when he fell. The slightest movement caused a spasm. He swallowed a sip of liquid tasting of copper, knowing the bite wound was still bleeding. Silence. Mac waited, watching Hayley. Mel was watching her too, also still and silent. Hayley looked up. Looked from Mac to Mel and back. She licked her lips.

"Well?" she asked.

Mac didn't speak, letting the silence become a lead weight pressing down on Hayley.

"Do I need a solicitor? I think I should have one," she said in a rush.

"Not if you have nothing to hide," Mel said quietly. "But I can call someone if you like?"

"Union rep?" Mac suggested.

Hayley shot him a look. Mac noticed a slight bruising on Hayley's neck, low down and only visible because she wasn't wearing a suit with a collared blouse. He'd put the bruise there amidst the throes of passion and lust. This was a novel experience. He'd never interviewed a suspect after sleeping with them. It made him feel acutely uncomfortable, but he hid any outward signs. He hadn't exploited her. They'd both wanted it, and he'd had no reason to suspect her of anything at that point. Still, Reid would go through the roof.

"If that SD card is Neill Smilley's, it's entirely accidental. I picked up the camera and felt the SD card on the floor. I retrieved it, thinking it was mine, not wanting to broadcast my clumsiness any more than I already had. What would you have done if you found the forensic pathologist working your case for you was such a clumsy butterfingers? Would it have inspired confidence, or would you have sent for Doctor Stringer? This was my big chance to work with Serious Crimes. And with you, Mac. You're a legend for the cases you've worked."

Mac would not be flattered. Nor was he going to fall for the wide-eyed, lip biting innocence of her expression.

"We'll get Mr. Smilley to identify his property. Until we can, I'm going to have you taken to Brunswick Street and held there for twenty-four hours. Mel, can you organise that, please?"

"Brunswick Street? That's in Edinburgh. For chrissakes, I've got work to do. I live in Inverness, you can't…"

Mac held up a hand. "I can. You're being held on suspicion of perverting the course of justice. This location doesn't come equipped with cells that conform with the European Court of Human Rights mandated minimum custody requirements. I could have you held in Inverness but I'm going to Edinburgh and I want to talk to you again. So, that's where you're going. If you're innocent we'll put you on a train afterward."

Mac stood, and Hayley followed suit. "Mac, please," she

caught his arm, holding on tight. "I thought…you know…
that we had something."

It was a last, desperate roll of the dice. Mac knew it.
"We don't. We had an enjoyable night together, but now
you're a person of interest in this investigation. If you have
a complaint about my conduct, DI Barland will give you the
relevant number to call for the Police Complaints
Commission."

He gently but firmly removed her hand from his sleeve
and walked past her. Hayley sat back down with a thud.
Mac didn't look back. As he stepped outside he saw one of
the local uniforms arriving for their shift. He waved her
over.

"I have a suspect under arrest inside. We're going to
transport her to Edinburgh. Sit in with her for now while DI
Barland arranges everything. She's a flight risk but we're not
cuffing her. Just be alert."

The PC nodded, heading inside and closing the door
behind her. There was the sound of the lock clicking into
place. Mac took out his phone, tapping out a message
to Mel.

"Escort her to HQ. Be her friend. Find out what you
can. And take care of the head. Organise Stringer."

He got a thumbs up within a few seconds. Then he
called Kai as he strode to his car.

"Kai, I've got a job for you and Isla. I need a deep background check on Doctor Hayley Blackwood, forensic
pathologist based in Inverness. Everything you can find out.
We're bringing her down today and I'd like a full dossier on
her before I go back into the interview room."

"Right, guv, will do. Got some info for you on Isabella
North and those two girls. They went to Edinburgh. Picked

them up on cameras on the M8 eastbound, passing Harthill, then joining the city bypass southbound."

"Any idea where they went?" Mac said sitting down in the car and picking up the duffel bag he'd left locked in there.

"Last sighted at the Craighall Interchange, heading toward Musselburgh. We've been going through highways agency cameras along that way but haven't picked them up again. Does Lowe have any properties out that way?"

"Probably," Mac said. "But they won't be in his name if he does. Drop it for now. Concentrate on Hayley Blackwood," Mac said.

"Right, guv," Kai replied. "Oh, one more thing, guv…"

Kai's voice was bright and chatty, like he was talking to one of his mates instead of his boss. Kai actually laughed as though about to tell a joke.

"You'll never guess who I bumped into this morning. Oh god…" he chuckled and Mac gritted his teeth, ready to explode.

There were sounds of movement followed by a door shutting. Then Kai was speaking but quieter and with clipped efficiency.

"Guv, sorry, had to get out of the office. I was contacted by Nari. On my personal phone. Had to take the call in the lavvy, so I didn't wake up…erm, actually, that doesn't matter. She wants to talk to you. She wouldn't say about what, but she said you're about to be thrown under the bus and she wants to help."

Mac froze, staring out of the windscreen, one hand on the duffel bag. He hadn't spoken to Nari since signing her transfer authorisation to DCI Akhtar's command. Nor had Nari reached out to him.

"She said that Akhtar is out for blood. Told me to remember who her uncle is?" Kai continued.

"Detective Chief Superintendent Omar Akhtar heads up an AC unit down south," Mac swore, closing his eyes.

Kai swore too, seeing the meaning behind Nari's coded message. Anti-Corruption were sniffing around. Every copper hated and feared them. They could end your career and cut off your pension. And you didn't always have to be guilty of something to fall under suspicion.

"Thanks, Kai," Mac didn't need to tell his sergeant to keep the news to himself.

"Good luck, guv," Kai sounded heartfelt.

# Chapter 18

**M**ac got out of his Audi on a car park of potholes and crumbling concrete. A tall fence, backed by rampant bamboo, screened the area from the road. Beyond it was a building that resembled an old farmhouse at its core. Around that structure were multiple recent additions. A faded rectangle at the front was the relic of signage that had proclaimed a different purpose for this building than the one it had now. McNeill thought it looked like a carvery pub. Farmhouse to carvery to women's refuge. Nothing announced the current purpose, which, he supposed, was exactly the point. He was back in his personal uniform. Open collared white shirt, dark suit, and overcoat. After the mud, rain, and woods of the highlands, he was glad to have an unyielding surface beneath his feet. He leaned back against the bonnet of the car, not approaching the building, knowing he wouldn't be allowed in. This was the kind of job that Melissa Barland was better suited to, but this was a name given to Reid by his informant. Reid was jealous of that informant. So, Mac waited for a woman abused by men for most of her life and who was probably extremely mistrustful.

He didn't see a door open, but a woman was suddenly walking towards him from one of the building's white painted wings. She wore a baggy cardigan clamped around her body from tightly folded arms, with crocks on her feet and a pinched expression. As she got nearer, he saw the scar that marked her from left ear to left nostril. His eyes went to hers and didn't go back to the scar. He knew she must be used to people staring and didn't want to add to any stereotypes she might have built up in her head.

"You the copper?" she said.

"DCI McNeill," Mac said.

"Who's your boss then?"

"Detective Chief Superintendent Reid. Kenny," Mac replied.

She came closer, taking cigarettes from a pocket of her cardigan and shaking one loose in Mac's direction. He took it and put it in his mouth, waiting for a light. She provided it and then lit one for herself.

"What do I call you?" Mac said.

"Maggie."

"Reid tells me you can give me some information about Isabella North and John Lowe," Mac said through a blue cloud.

"I used to work for her, didn't I?" Maggie said.

She had a remnant of London in her accent, overlaid with Edinburgh. It was a bizarre combination. Her mouth bore lines around it and her eyes seemed permanently set into a suspicious squint.

"As what?"

"Tom," she replied.

"And now?"

"I run this place. Women's refuge. I got out after this happened to me. Almost died. I was lucky."

Mac nodded somberly. "Did a punter do that to you?"

Maggie sneered. "Tried to. But I got the blade off him and turned it on him. Isabella did this to me as a punishment. The punter had a bit of money, eh? I was a bit younger then. Isabella was new to Johnny, still had the shine on. And she was putting her authority on the girls. Unlucky for me, eh?"

"So, Isabella was violent with the girls?" Mac said.

Maggie nodded. "She was a...what do you call it? Someone who gets off on pain?"

"Sadist," Mac offered.

"Aye, that's it. Proper one, she was. All the girls ended up more scared of her than they was of Johnny. He was a proper gent before he met her. Treated us good...well, for a pimp anyway. But after she came along..."

Maggie shook her head, taking a long drag and blowing out a twin smoke stream through her nostrils. She held the cigarette between thumb and forefinger, flicking the ash clear of the glowing tip. Mac's cigarette stuck out between his fingers, hand covering his mouth when he took a drag. Tasted like crap. Cheap ciggies. Like smoking dead skin. He suppressed an irritated cough which rose in protest from his throat.

"How did they get on?" he asked.

"You couldn't tell. When they were getting on they took lumps out of each other for fun. When they fell out they took lumps out of each other out of spite. Look, your boss wanted to know about them but I can tell you a lot more if you're interested. If you only want to talk about those two then I'm away. I'm not getting killed for spilling the T about their messed up relationship. But if you want some proper dirt, stuff that makes it worth the risk of talking to you…"

Mac frowned, drawing on the cigarette. He had only been looking to find out about Lowe and Isabella. Looking for a motive for Lowe to have her killed. And killed with such prejudice. Shot, beheaded, and fed to wolves. Mutilated after death. That didn't happen without a hate capable of burning a person from the inside out. Maggie rushed into the pause, throwing away her cigarette.

"Look, that other fella didn't want to know. So, I'm not expecting much from the old bill. If you're the same as him then you're wasting my time."

"Who?" Mac asked.

"Black fella. Big un. Moses or something," Maggie said.

"Musa?" Mac asked.

"That's him. Spoke to him, gave him everything I knew. And I know a lot. Never heard from him again. But one of the girls got a right doing over. That was a message to me, weren't it?"

"I don't work for or with Benjamin Musa. I'm on a different investigation. And I'm looking to take down John Lowe. If you can help then I promise you something will be done with the information," Mac said.

Maggie spat. "I trust Kenny Reid. He's a bit rough, but he's a good sort. And I've known him for years. Back when I was a lot younger, and he was a lot better looking. He says I can trust you and that's the only reason I'm talking to you."

"I understand," Mac said.

His heart was racing. An instinct that was rarely wrong was telling him that this was the loose thread. Pull it and a whole mess of knots would begin to unravel. It was a way in. He didn't know what Maggie had on John Lowe or how she was still alive, but he knew it must be significant.

"Before Isabella came along I was helping to run things down at the Port. I was like a courier, weren't I? You know like when you go to Spain and they tell you what bus to get on at the airport and stuff?"

"Port? You mean Leith?" Mac asked.

"Aye, down there. I handed out the papers to the girls and got them organised for where they were going. Some went into town. Some went to Glasgow, poor buggers, some went elsewhere."

"So John Lowe was trafficking people. Women?"

"Mostly. Some gays. Mostly girls. Isabella took it over, sent me back to the streets in Stenhouse, the cow. Almost got me killed."

Mac couldn't understand why DCI Musa wouldn't want to act on this woman's information. Unless, he was bent. Unless Supercop was in Lowe's pay and had just gone back to him and told him what he'd found out. If so, Maggie was lucky to be alive.

"How are you still here?" he asked, somewhat incredulous.

That got him the first smile from her. It went some way to light up her life hardened features.

"I got myself some protection, didn't I? I'm sure Johnny sent someone after me but the thing about this place is everyone here is hiding. Maggie isn't my real name and if you turn out to be bent like the other guy, I'll just disappear. Right after I get my friend to cut your balls off for you."

Mac grinned mirthlessly, dropping his cigarette, and crushed it beneath his shoe.

"I'm straight as they come, Maggie. Can't speak for Musa, one way or the other."

"Bent in both ways, mate," Maggie said, lighting another.

She offered a second to Mac, and he waved it away.

"Keep it, they're not cheap these day," he said. "How do you know Musa's gay?"

"Likes 'em young," Maggie said. "And you're the first person I've let on to that I know that. Apart from him. He knows that if anything happens to me, his secrets go public by my friend. My knight in shining armour."

She grinned, showing discoloured teeth and a gap. So, she'd helped Lowe run his prostitutes and had found out about DCI Musa's predilections, filing the evidence in a safe place. Musa may well be protecting her from on high with a threat like that over his head. Scared to kill her or ask Lowe to do it. He admired her courage.

"You might be interested to know that Isabella North is dead," Mac said.

Maggie laughed, clapping her hands together. "Seriously?" she demanded.

"About as serious as it gets. Shot, head cut off and the rest of her fed to a pack of wolves. There's nothing left. What they didn't consume they buried and we can't get near them to find any remains. She's gone."

Maggie swore in awe, shaking her head. "She must have really ticked off Johnny Lowe."

"You think he would kill her?" Mac asked.

"Aye, if she made him angry enough. That's how they were."

"I found out that Isabella was bringing two new girls in from Glasgow Airport. Ukrainians. Not smuggled, they came in on refugee passports. They ended up dead alongside Isabella. Shot. I'm trying to trace their movements. I know Isabella took them to the Craighall Interchange. Any idea where they'd be going?"

"If they weren't brought into the country in the shipping containers, then they'd be high-value girls. For the rich punters. Probably taken to the Grange."

"The Grange?" Mac asked, putting his hands in his trouser pockets.

"It's what they call this big old house out Musselburgh way. He put his mum there until she died. On a private beach down by a big golf course. Got his own dock for his boat."

Mac didn't think the Grange would be difficult to find, given the description. He was starting to wonder whether Lowe needed to be fitted up for Isabella North's death. It was looking more and more like a contract taken out on his own girlfriend. Except for the four lines carved into the body of the tree. And the inscription at the church. Those things meant something. And it just didn't fit with a simple contract to eliminate a woman Lowe was tired of, but who knew too much to just be dumped. If Sofia and Katya could be linked to this Grange and the Bartosz couple found to have provided sponsorship for their visas fraudulently, he could start to build a case against Lowe. It might not pin the murders on him, but attacking his people smuggling operation might just persuade someone else in the organisation to jump ship. More threads would unravel and the whole shebang could come apart.

After leaving the refuge he called Mel. There were more threads now than he could keep track of by himself. She'd come back to Edinburgh after successfully arranging for Stringer to go over Hayley Blackwood's forensic findings and put Isabella North's head on ice for him.

"Mel, I want you to visit Mr. and Mrs. Bartosz. I was planning to go myself but I have other fish to fry. Take Isla with you for backup, maybe a van as well in case you need to make an arrest. Push them on Sofia and Katya and see how they react. See if they're willing to flip on Lowe. Play it by ear."

"Right, guv. Isla's got the address. I'll get some uniform support. Where are you going to be?"

"I'm following up on a lead one of Reid's snouts gave me. I've got something, but I'm not talking about it on the phone, eh? I'm going to send you a text. Delete it after you read it," Mac said.

"Geez, guv. Watch many spy movies lately?"

"You'll see. Don't read it where anyone can see it."

Mac hung up, knowing he sounded paranoid, but not sure how far he could trust Isla McVey. If her boss was bent, then that made his team suspect. It didn't necessarily follow that the corruption went beyond Musa, but he couldn't take the chance. He rapidly fired off a message.

"Monitor IM. Superman poss bent."

Hardly an unbreakable code but better than just saying it straight out. And it would put Mel on her guard without Isla knowing. The next call that Mac made was to Nari Yun.

## Chapter 19

Seafield smelt of the nearby waterworks. The odour mixed with the ozone tang of the North Sea. A long stretch of road was bordered by a thin beach on one side and an industrial estate on the other. In a car park above the beach was a van selling burgers, hotdogs, and coffee. Mac saw Nari standing with a cup in her hand, leaning on a rusty railing and looking out to sea. He purchased a cup of his own from the van. The smell of instant coffee and ages old grease was mildly preferable to the smell of water being treated. He approached Nari, who didn't look around. Her dark hair was cut severely short at the back and sides, the top kept long and tied back. She glanced at him, eyes large, dark, and expressive. Nari had always been a serious one. Studious and diligent when she had been a member of his team. Now, he thought he could see lines in her face that hadn't been there before.

"Pleasant spot," he commented, sipping the coffee and grimacing.

"Didn't want to meet anywhere you'd normally be associated with," Nari said. "Plus it's out of the way enough that it's easy to spot a tail."

Mac leaned on the railing, cup held between his hands to warm them. There was a breeze coming off the sea that cut like a razor. His coat, rarely buttoned, gusted around him. Nari was wrapped up in a scarf and gloves.

"So, how are things with DCI Akhtar?" Mac asked.

Nari sighed deeply. "I'm sorry, guv. I made a mistake. I know it now. I just thought…she's a woman and a woman of colour. It seemed like she was a good bet for my career. Like she was going places."

"Thank you for the honesty," Mac said, drily.

"I should have been upfront with you about it. I messed up," Nari said.

There was genuine contrition in her voice. Mac glanced at her, saw the twisting of her face. It was hard to forget that she had gone behind his back.

"Akhtar got it wrong, but she's an honest copper," Mac said.

"She is. She got transferred to AC and I've transferred with her. Kind of like what Reid did with you."

Mac grunted. "I got shot to earn that privilege."

"I wanted to make up for getting it wrong before. Hafsa doesn't know I'm here."

"So, is Akhtar investigating me or Reid," Mac said, wanting to cut right to the meat.

"Reid. They're coming at him hard this time. No side-stepping. No politics."

"Why are you telling me? If he's under investigation then go for him. Nothing to do with me," Mac said.

"I wanted to give you a chance. I thought I owed you that much."

"A chance to distance myself from Reid," Mac said, not asking a question.

"Yes, and to help."

Mac tossed his rancid coffee away, dropping the cup into an overflowing bin nearby.

"Good to see you again, Nari. Good luck," He turned away.

This had happened before. AC sniffing around Reid and wanting to co-opt his closest confidante. There would be threats if Mac didn't respond to the entreaty. Once it had come from AC officers, bullies who thought they were above other officers. Now it came from a familiar face. And Nari expected him to believe that Hafsa Akhtar hadn't put her up to it.

"I'm risking my job for you, you bloody idiot!" Nari called after him.

Mac stopped, looked back over his shoulder. She was facing him. Looked angry. She was taking out her phone and striding towards him.

"Can we talk in your car? I've got something to show you."

She didn't wait for his answer but walked towards the Audi and stood beside the passenger door. Mac shrugged and followed her, unlocking the door with a hand in his coat pocket. The car beeped and Nari got in, slamming the door behind her. Mac got into the driver's seat.

"That door closed, yeah?" he said, sarcastically.

Nari hit the button for the radio, which came on in CD mode. Mayhem filled the enclosed space, sounding like deranged punk demons. She winced but didn't touch the volume, held out her phone towards him. Mac looked at the screen. It was a bank statement with Kenny Reid's name at the top. Mac's stomach sank as he noted the regular payments of four-figure sums going into the account. He scrolled through the transactions. Once a month. Then the same amount being moved somewhere else. Nari took the phone back. Mac turned the volume down enough for conversation. It sounded muted to him, but to anyone else, it would still be loud.

"He's on the take. We don't know where this money is coming from, but this is an undeclared bank account not shared with Police Scotland for normal audit purposes. You can see here, money comes in from a numbered account. It's in Bermuda. We haven't been able to trace anything yet. But, it seems suss, yeah?"

Mac nodded curtly, looking away. Reid had told him he was in hock to John Lowe through an investment trap. A property deal that turned out to be a fake left him owing money and vulnerable to blackmail. But this was different. Money being paid regularly to Reid from a secret offshore account. Payments for services rendered?

"How long have those payments been going to him?" Mac asked.

"A year," Nari replied. "Right about the time John Lowe went from bit player on the organised crime scene to rock star. Coincidence?"

"Right about the time Benjamin Musa's Organised Crime Taskforce was set up," Mac murmured.

He glanced at Nari, who frowned.

"Musa? He's been decorated. The George Cross."

"Something a snout told me, that's all," Mac said with a shrug. "I don't have any hard evidence. Not like you have there on Reid."

"Hafsa would say you're trying to deflect attention from your mentor," Nari said.

"Just passing on information. Want me to do it through official channels?" Mac said.

There was no possibility of that. It could get Maggie killed, and he'd decided he quite liked the old warrior. She was milking a corrupt cop and using the money to help women who needed it. There were worse ways of exploiting men.

"Not without proof. I wouldn't want to be investigating Musa unless I knew I was onto something. He's too well connected," Nari said.

"Very smart. You'll go far," Mac replied with a smirk.

Nari made an exasperated sound. "OK. I've put my neck on the line to try and make up for going behind your back. But I did nothing criminal, did I? I just put my career ahead of yours. Is that so bloody bad? But if you want to cut me off for it, go ahead. I've tipped you off. My job is in your hands. I thought you might appreciate the gesture...sir."

She opened the door.

"Nari," Mac said.

She paused, door half open.

"I apologise," he said finally. "You're right. I've been holding a grudge because you injured my pride. I know the risk you're taking here. Thank you."

Nari smiled. It was weak and harassed but she accompanied it by squeezing his hand where it rested on the gear stick.

"I know how difficult it is for you to say that."

Mac laughed. "Not too difficult these days. Only like pulling off my skin."

"You've been listening to too much of this death stuff," Nari replied.

"Thrash, not death," Mac corrected.

"Try Taylor Swift."

Mac barked out a genuine laugh at the thought. Nari grinned.

"I actually miss you, guv," she said.

"Aye, you too. You were one of my best. You'll be a DCI before you know it. I mean it."

Nari nodded. "Mum's in a flat in Airdrie living off universal credit. Dad worked himself into an early grave. I just want to be a success."

"Your dad's dead?" Mac said, more bluntly than he had intended.

"Last year. Heart attack. The business was on the skids. He was supposed to be the boss, but he was doing most of the driving by the end."

There was a look in Nari's eyes that said she should be crying, as though there was nothing left.

"Were you close?" Mac realised he didn't know, had never known.

"Not lately. He was working so much. Always away on the road. And my mum…" Nari laughed, bitterly. "I can't stand her attitude. She won't work and she's surrounded by people just like her. I tried to persuade her to move out to Edinburgh, even move in with me. But she won't. I don't think she's ever worked in her life. It was always my dad breaking his back to make ends meet. That's why I joined the force. To make something of my life."

"I didn't know," Mac said, softly.

He felt shame that he'd never taken the time to find out. He knew Nari's skills as a police officer, as a detective. Didn't know about her as a person. And he'd rushed to judge her when she'd wanted to transfer out of his team. He'd been so full of himself, ego so bruised at the thought that anyone would not want to work for him. But those words were locked inside. Clio could have released them. Annika Eklund had drawn him out through sheer, brutal directness. But, they were exceptions. He gripped the steering wheel, staring ahead with teeth gritted behind a straight mouth.

"For what it's worth, guv. Hafsa might be a cold, heartless politician. But she asked. That was one of the reasons I transferred."

Mac nodded. The words bubbled up, and he opened his mouth, but Nari was already out of the car.

"Good luck, guv," she said, not knowing that she was echoing Kai's words earlier.

She closed the door and walked away.

"Everyone is telling me that lately," Mac muttered, watching her go.

"Bloody eejit," he added, not meaning Nari.

Then his thoughts went to Reid. A cold anger frosted over his insides. Three murders and Reid was throwing a spanner in the works by taking bribes. He'd lied to Mac in order to get himself out of hock to John Lowe. Kept back the depth of his corruption until when? Until Mac was in too deep? And the old bastard knew all along he'd been taking backhanders. Mac slammed the palm of his hand into the steering wheel. Again. Rage seethed in him. It wasn't cold anymore. It was volcanic. With teeth bared, he gripped the wheel, fingers digging in. He wanted to hit someone. Wanted to hurt someone. Prying his hand from the wheel, he turned up the music, higher even than he usually liked. A song with a name that summoned the most unpleasant images buzzed at the low end, speakers unable to cope with the bass levels. Mac knew the anger demanded fed. That if he let it, it would consume him. This was no different from the panic attacks induced by rain, awakening memories of Skye and Iona. Dan Hendry described it as gases bubbling up from a festering mass within him. Mac suspected he'd picked his analogy after establishing the kind of music Mac was into. Different gases were produced by that black mass of trauma. Some made him afraid. Some made him angry. All crippled him in some way or another.

The panic came from the memories of Iona. The anger was directed at her killer. None of it was in the present. Mac was. He was alive. The music was present. The pain in his fingertips was present. The smell of Edinburgh's sewage was present. He took a deep breath, imagining the cold air suppressing the fire of that anger. Another. He closed his eyes as the riffs of Freezing Moon reverberated within him, making his head nod in time with the insanely aggressive tune. Distortion that rendered every touch of the guitar strings an almost incomprehensible mess of sharp-edged sounds. But suppressing the sharp edges within himself. Mac opened his eyes and took out his phone, dialling Reid's number and shutting off the music. The sudden silence was as jarring as a sudden noise. It didn't last long. A sound reached him from outside. A clap of thunder that made him flinch. There was no sign of it in the sky. No lightning, no storm. The sky was light grey, but the ground was dry. Christ! Not thunder. An explosion.

# Chapter 20

**R**eid didn't answer. The call went straight to voicemail. Mac left one.

"Sir, we need to talk. You know what about."

Cold, emotionless. In control. He would get answers from his boss and then decide if he wanted to cut ties. There was still something Reid had that Mac wanted. Something he had the power to grant. Dan Hendry had talked a lot about unresolved trauma. Using the hatefully transatlantic, hipster word, closure. Talked about visiting Skye, seeing what was left of his home. Reducing it in his mind from the spectre that it currently was. Saying goodbye to Iona. Mac couldn't see how that would help. Had no desire to cry over the loss of the McNeill farmhouse or leave flowers on the spot where Iona's body was found. There was only one way he knew to achieve closure on an unsolved murder. To solve it. He tossed the phone onto the passenger seat and left the car park, heading west into the sprawling city.

He had heard sirens as he was passing through

Lochend. A lot of sirens. There were always emergency vehicles blaring their warnings in a city like Edinburgh. It was white noise to anyone living in a metropolis. But this was more than usual. Mac's ears pricked at an unconscious instinct telling him that something major was going on. Probably a road traffic accident. A multi-vehicle pile-up somewhere. His eye was caught by the yellow and blue helicopter that darted overhead, briefly visible in the gap between rundown tenements and anonymous brick high rises. No one on the streets of Lochend looked up, but Mac noted the direction of its flight. North. He turned onto Lochend Road, heading in that direction towards Leith. The helicopter appeared overhead before disappearing behind a skyline from which an ancient church surged, standing shoulder to shoulder with a high-rise. The road was clear for the time of day and he put his foot down. Flashing blue lights came roaring up from behind, swerving out to overtake and then racing through the junction with Easter Road.

His own flat was just around the corner. The lights changed he floored the accelerator and followed the wailing police car. More blue lights from Easter Road. An ambulance with a police car in front. Lights strobing. Sirens full blast. This was more than just a pile up. As he raced along Great Junction Street towards Junction Bridge, he saw the plume of smoke staining the sky. It was thick and black, boiling up from somewhere north of the Leith Water. From the port. Northbound traffic was thickening ahead of him now, but the opposite side of the road was clear. Mac swerved onto the right-hand side of the road, keeping his foot flat and tearing past the tailback leading to the bridge. A car coming the other way slammed on, hammering his horn, and Mac nipped back into the left, at the head of the queue, with a few feet to spare. More lights behind the snarl up now. At least two emergency vehicles taking the same route Mac had just used. Civilian drivers joined the tumult with horns. Beside him, his phone was suddenly ringing.

He didn't look but stabbed the button on the steering wheel that answered calls hands-free.

"McNeill!" he shouted.

"Guv, are you ok?" Mel answered. "Where are you?"

"What the hell is going on, Mel?" Mac barked. "I can see smoke coming from Leith harbour and a lot of blues and twos."

"There's been an explosion at the port. At a container depot. Everything with flashing lights has been scrambled there. Chief Superintendent Hawley's been assigned Gold Commander for the incident and he's been trying to get DCS Reid."

"I can't get him either. Is there any indication of the cause yet?"

"Not yet. From the 999 calls the story seems to be that a container exploded and there are bodies at the scene."

"Shit. Tell Hawley I'm practically on site. Keep trying Reid. If this turns out to be deliberate SCU will need to be involved."

"Understood. Wait. Just had an update through from Gold Command. The explosion happened at the north-west corner of the Western Harbour."

"There's a container port there. Christ, the Britannia is just over the water. We'll be up to our necks in MI5."

Mac made an instant call, swerving wildly into oncoming traffic to dive into a side street barely large enough to accommodate the Audi. It rattled and bumped along the uneven ground but came out on a residential street. It was one way, and he wasn't going in the right direction, but emerged from it before anything else turned in. He drove a switchback path through traffic calming and one-way systems until the Audi screamed into Newhaven Road. He clenched his teeth against the rattle of the cobbles. The road was a canyon between old Edinburgh tenements, stained black. One side gave way to lockups. A bang to one side announced a wing mirror clipped. Glancing in that direction, he saw his was intact, but something was bouncing on the road behind him from the impact. Ahead was open sky and then the sea. As he slowed towards the junction, he saw the towering column of smoke, alive with fire at its base, off to one side. He drove in that direction. A perimeter had been established by first responders, police cars blocking the road. Mac showed his ID and was waved through.

He stopped behind a line of ambulances. Fire fighters were at the front line, getting their gear in place to fight the fire. Mac could see the conflagration was contained within a yard, shipping containers stacked within and trucks parked in ranks opposite. The sign on the wall surrounding the yard was Lowe Shipping. Mac stopped, one hand on the open door of the car, staring at that sign. He'd rushed to the scene driven by the instinct of a copper faced with an emergency. Now it was as though he was meant to be here. This couldn't be a coincidence. John Lowe was under attack. His girlfriend murdered. His dealers picked off one by one. And now this. A business Mac assumed was legit, a front to explain his money while also probably serving as a gateway into the UK for people and drugs smuggling. His eyes fell on paramedics running back through the line established by the firefighters, carrying a body on a stretcher. There were others just outside the gates, lying still. The emergency service personnel were risking the licking flames to run forward and help those people.

Mac's first instinct was to join them but he knew he'd be more of a hindrance now the first responders were here. It was only by chance that he looked around at the same time DCS Kenny Reid was loaded, strapped to a stretcher, into the back of an ambulance.

"Sir!" he called, racing forward.

A paramedic was about to close the doors when Mac flashed his warrant card.

"That's my guvnor," he said.

"He's unconscious. Second-degree burns and smoke inhalation. We dragged him out of the yard," the paramedic told him.

Mac registered that the man had a soot blackened face and a rasp to his voice, like he'd had his own share of smoke inhalation.

"You coming with us?" the man demanded; hand still on the ambulance door.

"Which hospital?" Mac asked.

"Western General, mate."

Mac stepped back, and the doors were slammed shut. He looked around at a scene that resembled a war zone. If Kenny Reid had been here, then maybe... He began looking around, jogging to the next ambulance into which a casualty was being loaded. Each time he flashed his warrant card, got a look at the injured man or woman, and moved on. None of them wore Hi-Viz. If they were workers here, he'd have expected them all to be wearing it. They looked to be dressed raggedly, a mismatch of clothes that were clearly not new. Men and women, all young, in their twenties, maybe though it was hard to tell under the soot. He stopped in front of one man, breathing heavily into an oxygen mask, shivering uncontrollably under a foil blanket as shock set in. Mac crouched in front of him, ignoring the protests of the attending paramedic.

"Hey!" he snapped his fingers in front of the man's face.

"He's concussed!" the paramedic said.

"Look at me!" Mac insisted. "I'm police. Do you work here?"

The man shook his head, eyes wide, chest heaving as he sucked in oxygen.

"No, I didn't think so. How did you get here?" Mac demanded.

The man pointed towards the yard. "Ship," he said, voice muffled by the mask.

"In a container?" Mac asked.

The man looked at him blankly. Maybe container wasn't a word he'd learned yet.

"In one of those?" Mac pointed to the shipping containers in the yard which had been scattered like Lego.

The man nodded. Mac straightened. The paramedics glared at him.

"Hey! You! Copper!" a voice yelled.

Mac turned and saw John Lowe walking away from a paramedic towards him. His face was blackened and his forehead was bleeding profusely. Under the soot and the blood was a face twisted into rage. He pointed, finger shaking.

"You! Copper! Get here now!"

Mac bared his teeth briefly, hands flexing and the anger he had so recently suppressed and dispersed, returned at the arrogance of the summons. A uniform PC had seen Lowe approaching Mac and moved to step between them. Lowe thrust the man aside with surprising strength, making him stagger. The PC came back with immediate escalation, reaching for Lowe's arm to twist it and restrain him if need be. Lowe turned to him; spit flying from his mouth as he hurled abuse at the PC.

"It's OK officer. I can handle this," Mac said, approaching.

The PC released Lowe and stepped back, breathing hard and glaring daggers. He had no clue who Lowe was. Mac wanted to make sure Lowe never found out who the PC was. He jerked his head towards the Audi.

"Over here. You don't look like you need immediate hospital treatment. Have a chat, eh?"

He turned his back on Lowe who snarled his outrage.

"Don't you turn your back on me, pal! I own you!"

Mac ignored him, reaching the car and getting in. Lowe stood for a minute, impotent with anger and then followed. He got in next to Mac who immediately started the engine and drove away, slowly navigating the emergency vehicles and personnel. Beyond the police cordon he put his foot down, heading away from the scene in a random direction, keeping the sea to his right.

"You kidnapping me now, yeah?" Lowe said.

Mac opened the glove box and took out a packet of tissues.

"Here, for your head," he said, tossing it onto Lowe's lap.

"What are you and Reid playing at? Someone is trying to kill me. That's my outfit back there! Someone is having a go at my family and my business. You're supposed to be doing something about it."

They were heading along the coast, north of Pilton. Ahead were the sandflats connecting Cramond Island to the mainland at low tide. The road was quiet, trees screening it from the housing estates beyond.

"Where are you taking me, pal?" Lowe demanded.

Mac shifted in his seat and smacked Lowe in the mouth with the back of his hand. As Lowe's hands went up to his face, Mac grabbed the back of his head and rammed it forward, smashing his forehead into the dashboard. Lowe hadn't bothered to put on his seat belt. Blood gushed from his nose.

"Don't get that on my upholstery," Mac said, casually.

Lowe put up his hands to catch the blood. Mac pulled over suddenly, tyres skidding as he pulled into a gravel layby on the sea-side of the road. There was a drop of around seven or eight feet from the layby to rocks below, from which a shingle beach extended to the surf. Mac got out and strode around the car. Lowe's eyes were wide as he kicked the door open on his side. Mac kicked it shut again as Lowe tried to get out. As the door bounced he caught it and swung it again. The anger had him by the throat now. His teeth were bared and his face contorted into an animalistic rage. Grabbing Lowe by the throat he dragged him to the edge of the layby and swung his upper body out over the drop. Anger had given way to stark terror in Lowe's face now.

"What makes you think I'm in your pocket? Pal!" Mac hissed. "Haven't you heard I got John Boy Allen off a murder charge once?"

He could see the blood draining from Lowe's face, where it wasn't hopelessly stained from the cut on his forehead or the broken nose Mac had given him.

"Tell me the truth or I drop you on your head and let Hance Allen pick apart your business. Is Kenny Reid on the take? I know how you entrapped him with the loan. I want to know if he works for you."

Lowe's eyes were wide and kept trying to slide away

towards the drop behind him. Not enough to definitely kill him, unless he landed on his head. Mac let his grip slacken, and Lowe slipped a few inches. He cried out, grabbing at Mac's hands with the ferocity of a drowning man.

"No! Ok! No!" he blabbered.

"I've seen the bank statements. Offshore payments going into his account. Who else would they come from?" Mac demanded.

"I had them faked! They're fakes! For fuck's sake pull me back!"

Mac let go with one hand. He leaned back as he did, feeling the strain in the one arm he held Lowe by. If Lowe had been a bigger man, he'd be falling by now. But Mac could just about hold on.

"It's true! He wasn't giving me what I wanted. I needed some leverage. To show him I meant business. Once he got the message my man inside the polis would make the fakes disappear. I swear it was just for blackmail. He refused to take a penny."

Mac's teeth were bared, the muscles in his left arm taut and singing with pain. His grip on Lowe's shirt was slipping. He looked into the man's eyes and saw the truth there. Mac pulled him back from the brink. For one horrifying moment he thought he'd waited too long, that he lacked the strength to pull him to safety. Then the momentum of his body kicked in and he just managed to hurl Lowe to the side, onto the straggly grass at the edge of the broken tarmac. Mac stepped back, breathing hard. Lowe's panic had evaporated. The look he shot Mac was that of a rabid predator.

"You're a dead man!" he hissed. "You're dead!"

"Better be quick," he said.

He stepped to Lowe and kicked him in the stomach. As

Lowe convulsed, Mac rifled his pockets, found his phone, and pocketed it.

"I think I saw a bus stop a mile back that way," he said, pointing. "By the time you get back to the city, the police will be racing the press to find you and ask questions about the dead illegals in your shipping containers."

He walked to the car and drove away. As he drove he wound the window down and tossed Lowe's phone out onto the road.

# Chapter 21

When Mac reached the Western General Hospital, Reid had already been triaged and moved to the burns unit. A doctor in blue scrubs, and a clipped manner that spoke of a bedside manner pared to the bone, denied him entry to the room Reid was being kept in. Mac could see his boss through the window, lying on a bed, one side of his face covered in clear plastic and angry red beneath. It looked like the hair on that side of his head had gone too. He looked small and frail. Mac's anger at him was replaced by guilt at believing he could be corrupt rather than just foolish. Reid was willing to cut corners to get the right result, and he would not have had a problem with Mac dropping Lowe. But he wouldn't take a bribe.

"He's under sedation, so he wouldn't be able to talk to you, anyway. But I can't risk infection at this stage, so he needs to stay in isolation."

The doctor spoke with impatient authority, half Mac's

height and skinny. But, impassable. Mac nodded, running a hand through his hair.

"Is he stable?" he asked.

"Yes, I would describe his condition as serious but stable. You're welcome to stay but he's going to be under for several hours. I'm sure you have better things to be doing."

Mac nodded. "Can I give you my number for when he wakes up? He has no family or wife. I don't know who else you would call."

"No next of kin?" the doctor frowned, glancing at a metal clipboard.

"If you have one on file it's out of date. I don't know who he'd put down these days."

"Ok, ok," the doctor said, taking out a pen.

Mac gave his name and number; the doctor scribbled them hastily on the clipboard and then left without a word. Mac watched him go into the room and hang the clipboard from the foot of Reid's bed, then hurry out and down the corridor. Mac looked up and down the hall. This section of the hospital didn't look frenetically busy, despite the harried body language of the doctor and the injuries at the port. He saw a door at the end of the corridor labelled family room and walked towards it. Empty. He went in and sat in an armchair with wooden arms and a plastic covered cushion. Putting his head back, the urge to close his eyes was almost unbearable. It was a response to trauma. He knew that. After being at the scene of the explosion with the first responders, he knew he would receive an invitation from Dr. Siddhu to talk through his experience.

That made him pick his head up, scrubbing a hand across his face. In his pocket, his phone buzzed insistently. He took it out. Kai.

"Guv, you OK? Mel told me you were at the scene of the explosion."

"Fine, thanks, mum," Mac said, standing up to stave off the wooliness in his head.

Kai snorted. "Yeah, right. OK, so I've done a background check on Doctor Blackwood. No record, but she is on the system. She gave a witness statement when a friend of hers OD'd in a night club back in 2022. Accused the friend's boyfriend of giving her the drugs. Of being a dealer, in fact. Drugs squad couldn't make it stick, though. No arrest made. There's a link in the file though to the boyfriend, one Jake Summers. Now, I think he was actually a dealer because in December last year he was abducted from his flat and tortured. Ended up with acid in his eyes. Real mess. No-one ever arrested for it but about a week after he was found, at a storage unit by the airport, Craig Kelly was killed. Then Sean Grant a week after that. All tortured first, mutilated. You know the script with those two."

Mac was staring out of the window of the family room, out over residential streets, rooftops, and chimneys. He took a deep breath.

"So Jake Summers isn't dead?"

"No, last known address is his parent's, Colinton."

"Isabella North's eyes were put out," Mac speculated aloud. "Craig Kelly and Sean Grant's weren't. Something she saw that she was being punished for? What did Jake Summers see? Something they both turned a blind eye to."

Kai remained quiet. He'd worked with Mac for long enough to know not to interrupt when his boss was thinking aloud.

"What was the name of the friend who took the overdose?" Mac asked, the thought popping into his head.

"Um…wait a sec…Lydia Webb," Kai said, accompanied by the sound of paper rustling.

The hairs on the back of Mac's neck stood up. LW.

"Do you have her date of birth there?" he asked.

"Sure, 17th of November…"

"2001," Mac finished for him.

So the inscription carved out in the church's stone was Lydia's initials and date of birth. Which made the man who carved them her father. Most likely. Neill Smilley's account said that he was a man. The SD card would verify that. A man who camped out in a derelict church and carved Lydia's initials and date of birth into the wall. Who else would do that but a father?

"Is that significant, guv?" Kai asked.

"Do you have names for Lydia's parents?" Mac asked, urgently.

"Angela Barnes and Daniel Webb." Kai recited.

"And Daniel Webb is ex-military," Mac said.

"I don't have that, guv. What makes you think so?"

"He's confident with firearms and he wears army gear. And Hayley Blackwood is ex-army too."

"Lydia Webb was in medical school. But Hayley Blackwood had graduated already. They didn't become friends at university."

"But Hayley might have known the father. She was an army medic. Meets Daniel Webb, maybe treats him. Meets the family, becomes friends with Lydia. Maybe she was Auntie Hayley? And that's why Hayley tried to cover up Daniel Webb's identity. She knew what he was doing and took her chance when she realised that Neill Smilley could identify Webb. Brave girl."

"Guv?"

"Never mind. We need to find this guy. He's punishing

the people he believes are responsible for his daughter's death. I'd bet that Sean Grant and Craig Kelly both gave drugs to Jake Summer to sell at some point. He gets their names from Summers, finds out from them who they work for. Then goes after Lowe. Targets Isabella North to punish him, scare him. Then goes after his business. Takes out the hub of Lowe's people smuggling operation. There were bodies in the shipping containers that got blown up."

"Christ!" Kai breathed. "So this guy has access to explosives."

"And knows how to use them," Mac said.

This moment was better than sex. Almost. The moment when all the disparate pieces of information clicked together. When everything made sense. It always seemed so obvious once the problem was solved. Mac always ended up kicking himself that he hadn't seen it sooner.

"We need to find Daniel Webb. I'm coming back to talk to Hayley. Track down the wife. I'm presuming they're separated if they're giving different names."

"Doesn't say but I'm thinking the same."

"Get onto Mel. She and Isla are on a goose chase now. Lowe's people smuggling is well and truly exposed. Oh, Christ…"

Mac was thinking of his encounter with Lowe. Of leaving him to walk miles back into Edinburgh from the outskirts. Alone. If everything Mac had just pieced together was correct, Daniel Webb's next step would be to take Lowe. Mac had to hope that he intended the final killing to be long and drawn out. A punishment rather than an execution.

"What is it, guv?" Kai asked.

"I just left Lowe to walk back from somewhere out by Cramond Island. Didn't even let him keep his phone."

Kai laughed. "You did what? Are you mental?"

"I think I was," Mac replied, unable to resist smiling.

"Maybe you should just step back and let this nutter have him? You'd be doing a lot of people a favour."

Mac knew Kai wasn't serious. Not entirely serious. But that was the devil whispering. That was how bent coppers started. Turn a blind eye when gangs discipline their own. When men like Hance Allen and John Lowe take retribution and rid the streets of a dealer or a nonce. Turn a blind eye because they're serving the same purpose as the police. They're just not shackled by the courts. That was how Strack had started. How Mac had started.

"No, he's going down for a long time. And he's going to live through it. Even a slow painful death is too easy for him," Mac said.

Kai sighed. "There's me hoping for an early finish tonight. I'll get hold of Mel and give her the lowdown."

"I'm coming in. Once I've spoken to Hayley Blackwood again I'll get the team together and we'll make a plan."

Mac realised at that moment that he didn't know how to get hold of John Lowe. He knew about the Grange. Maybe that's where Lowe would head for once he could get someone from his firm to pick him up. But there was no guarantee he'd choose that property. Or that he wouldn't be gunning for Mac and Reid now, throwing caution to the wind because he knew the noose was tightening. Mac felt he needed to try and get a message to Lowe. First, though, he needed to protect Reid. He called Fran Dryden, now South-East Division Commander. With Reid out of action, she would be the next in the chain of command and had the authority to assign police protection, as well as initiate a manhunt for John Lowe.

He also knew that Fran, while a stickler for protocol,

could also recognise when immediate action was needed. For that reason, she was often the first choice as Gold Commander when the brown stuff hit the fan. This time, she had been second to Gold Commander Hawley when the explosion happened. Mac just hoped she had some resources left. The call was brief and not entirely what he would have hoped for. A pair of PCs to stand guard on Reid's hospital room. No spare bodies to find John Lowe. He was on his own until the emergency was over. Dryden recognised the risk in allowing him to remain on the streets if his life was in danger, was conscious of how exposed she and the police would be if he were killed. But she would not put the welfare of a people smuggler above the lives of those injured by the explosion. That would be extraordinarily bad optics. Her words.

Mac waited at the hospital until two PCs arrived and gave them instructions before hurrying away, back to his car and Brunswick Street station. Hayley was in custody there, waiting out her twenty-four hours until she either had to be released or charged. Both she and he knew that the evidence he had was purely circumstantial. He couldn't prove that she hadn't thought the SD card she'd picked up was hers. Or that she had ejected it from the camera deliberately. Intent couldn't be proved. He put his head around the door of the office before heading down to the interview rooms. Kai was on the phone, as was Mel. Mac caught Isla's gaze briefly and beckoned her. It would be good for her to report back to Musa that Mac was pursuing an alternative theory about the killings of Grant and Kelly. That the Isabella North case was also not about organised crime.

"I need backup for an interview. Doctor Hayley Blackwood, we've got her downstairs. Did Kai or Mel bring you up to speed?"

"Yes, sir. I know who she is. DCI Musa has asked me to see if you're free for a meeting."

"Has he? No, too busy. And so are you. Come on."

Mac strode to the lifts, Isla following, suppressing a smile.

"How're you liking working for me?" Mac asked.

"It's a good team," Isla said, sounding as though she were being diplomatic.

"Not as high profile as Supercop," Mac said.

"Not as cutthroat either," Isla said.

The lift doors opened, and they got in.

"Cutthroat?"

"Musa likes to play us off against each other. Compete. It makes for some tense relationships."

"Whatever works for him," Mac said, noncommittally.

"Doesn't work particularly well for me," Isla muttered.

As they stepped out of the lift and headed for the interview rooms, Mac saw a tall figure coming in the opposite direction. Benjamin Musa was both taller than Mac and broader. His hair was clipped short, and he wore an expensive suit. He was snapping orders to another man walking alongside him who had to almost run to keep up. Then Musa's dark eyes alighted on Mac.

"DCI McNeill! The very man. I need to talk to you about the Isabella North case," Musa called out.

"Later, DCI Musa. I've got a suspect to interview and we're on the clock."

"That would be Hayley Blackwood, yes?" Musa said, trying to stop in front of Mac.

Mac sidestepped without missing a beat, forcing Musa to turn and follow. Or shout down the corridor.

"I've just been speaking to DCC Mayhew, and he thinks that your case should sit with my team. It clearly links to…"

"Nope. It doesn't." Mac said. "We have new information and this has nothing to do with organised crime. I know who killed Isabella North and your two dead drug dealers."

There was silence for a minute. Mac reached the interview room door and grasped the handle. Musa caught up and put his own hand on top of Mac's. Coal-black eyes bored into his.

"What are you saying?" he said, quietly.

"I'm saying that I'm about to wrap up my case and yours. Don't thank me."

"You're going against Mayhew's orders," Musa said.

Mac's response was to describe Mayhew in a single sexually explicit word. Musa grinned mirthlessly.

"OK, Mac," he put emphasis on the moniker as though considering it foolish. "Isla, I've got work for you to do."

"Isla's with me," Mac told him, opening the door and stepping aside for the DS to enter. "You assigned her to my team, remember? When she's available, I'll send her up."

Mac stepped in and closed the door in Musa's face.

# Chapter 22

**M**ac sat in front of Hayley and let Isla go through the preliminaries. A duty solicitor sat next to her, a woman with curly hair and a down-turned mouth in a round face. She gave Mac and Isla a brief smile. Mac recalled her from a couple of other interviews, but couldn't bring the name to his mind. She gave it for the benefit of the tape.

"Tell me about Daniel Webb," Mac said.

Hayley had been about to say something. Possibly ready to answer a question she had not yet been asked. But this seemed to give her pause. She looked at her solicitor, who looked back attentively.

"I don't…" Hayley began.

"You were friends with his daughter. You both served in the Army at the same time," Mac cut across her.

"The British Army's a big place."

"You knew Lydia," Mac persisted.

Hayley opened her mouth. Again, a glance at her solicitor and an attentive, patient look was returned. Mac got the impression that the solicitor knew nothing about Lydia or Daniel Webb and had thought herself defending a client arrested for perverting the course of justice.

"I did."

"How did you meet her?" Mac asked.

Hayley hesitated, looking down at the table. Mac felt some sympathy for her. How could he not? He had slept with her. That intimacy couldn't just be wiped from his mind. It wouldn't stop him from doing what was needed, but when she looked so vulnerable, he couldn't help but feel a little protective.

"It's not a difficult question. I just want to know how you met your friend Lydia Webb," Mac said, putting a hard tone into his voice.

Hayley looked up, eyes wide and moist. Mac made himself hold her gaze.

"I don't remember," Hayley said. "We just met on a night out."

"You're a bit older than she was," Mac pointed out. "You didn't meet at medical school. She was still in high school when you went to Edinburgh uni. And you were in the army when she started medical school."

"I told you. A night out. We got talking."

"You see, I think we're going to find that you and her father were on the same tour of duty. Afghanistan. Iraq maybe. I think he was wounded, and you treated him. Maybe you were on a battlefield," Mac speculated.

"That kind of thing establishes a powerful bond," Isla put in. "It's not uncommon for a bond such as that to continue beyond a shared tour of duty."

Mac didn't look away from Hayley, but he felt a surge of pride in the young sergeant. He hadn't had time to fully brief her on what he wanted to get out of Hayley, but she was very sharp, quick. Mac decided, as he waited for Hayley to respond, that he would ask her to transfer to his team. Regardless of whether Musa was exposed as...whatever he was, Mac wanted Isla working for him.

"Did you become involved in a sexual relationship with Daniel Webb?" Mac asked.

Hayley wouldn't meet his eye. Again she looked to her solicitor, then leaned over and whispered to her.

"I think the police are entitled to ask any questions they wish," the solicitor told her gently, but in a voice audible to the room and the tape.

Hayley sat back as though stung and folded her arms tightly about herself. She'd clearly thought that she couldn't be asked questions not directly linked to what she'd been arrested for. Mac liked the solicitor even more. Her name had already left his mind, but he resolved to remember it in the future. About time he came across some people good at their jobs and honest. Sometimes it felt like the entire world was either incompetent or corrupt. Or both.

"Your charge of perverting the course of justice hinges on the fact that you were trying to conceal the identity of the man we believe killed Isabella North and two others," Mac said.

"It's not unreasonable therefore to assume you knew their killer," Isla put in.

It was the perfect one-two punch, making Hayley look from one to the other and disorientating her. Mac continued.

"Otherwise why put your neck on the line to protect him."

"I don't know any..."

"We know several people connected to Lydia's overdose have either died or been severely injured. Punished," Mac leaned forward. "Jake Summers, Lydia's ex-boyfriend, was blinded with acid. Isabella North had her eyes removed. Two drug dealers murdered, two dealers that I think supplied drugs to Jake Summers and were targeted as a result. Daniel Webb has a motive. Revenge. He's ex-army. A marksman and skilled with explosives. You probably haven't heard, but a bomb was set off at the harbour earlier. A lot of people are dead or injured and property belonging to John Lowe was the target. Those dealers I mentioned? They were his boys."

"You're not going to be in any more trouble than you already are by talking to us," Isla put in, adopting a gentle, cajoling tone.

Mac didn't need to look at her to know she was smiling. The same motherly smile that Mel was so good at. Of course, Isla was a lot younger, so it would be more sisterly coming from her.

"You attended Lydia's funeral?" Mac asked.

Hayley nodded, looking down.

"For the tape, please," Mac said.

"Yes."

"Were her parents there?" Isla asked.

Hayley nodded. "Yes."

"Did you speak to them?" Mac asked.

"Yes! OK? Yes, I knew Danny. I knew him."

"We know," Mac replied. "How well did you know him?"

"We met in Afghanistan. Helmand," Hayley said. "My only tour. I couldn't go back and resigned my commission when it was over. He was SAS. He'd been wounded by an IED and was brought into the hospital I was working at, at the base. He was there for a few days and we got talking. He was separated from his wife, estranged from his daughter.

Desperate to win them both back but addicted to the service. It's not uncommon, especially among special forces. They like being part of an elite. The rest of the army look at them like they're gods."

"Were you romantically involved?" Isla asked.

Hayley nodded. "Briefly. I was traumatised by battlefield medicine. Totally unprepared. So I was vulnerable, and he was…lonely I guess. My tour ended before his and we didn't continue it. Just kept in touch from time to time on socials."

"But close enough that you got to know his daughter," Mac said.

"He asked me to look out for her. Said she was going to university in Edinburgh to study medicine, but he was worried about the people she was hanging about with. So was her mum. Jake Summers was a complete scumbag," Hayley practically spat his name. "So I got in touch with her. Said I was friends with her dad. Lydia was a sweet girl, just a bit naïve. Anyway, we became friends."

Mac sat back, seeing the floodgates now fully open and the words pouring out of Hayley. It was common. At first, that dam could be hard to crack, but eventually it always was. Once that happened, the flood just seemed to erode any resistance. That was when a suspect stopped thinking of getting away with it and started thinking about mitigation.

"How close were you?" Isla asked.

"We were like sisters. We got very close, quickly. She was using recreational drugs when I met her and I thought I'd helped her kick them. Then Jake came along," Hayley said. "He got her into them again. Started giving her freebies, ecstasy, stuff like that. She thought she needed them. She was struggling in her third year, couldn't find the time to get everything done. She thought she needed the speed to keep her going."

Tears appeared in Hayley's eyes and the solicitor wordlessly produced a tissue from her bag, which sat beside the table on the floor. Hayley dabbed at her eyes.

"Lydia had so much potential. Was compassionate, wanted desperately to be a doctor, to help people. She wanted to join Medicine sans Frontières, and work in war zones. Even after I told her the truth about being a combat medic, what it was really like. That was where there was the most need. She thought it would be a great adventure. Stupid girl! Stupid, stupid girl!"

Hayley broke down, her face crumpling and tears spilling down her cheeks. Mac stood before he knew what he was doing. The solicitor looked up startled as Mac went around the table and crouched beside Hayley. He gently took her hand in his own, putting his head close to hers.

"Lydia was driven, but she was full of impostor syndrome. Every time she failed, she beat herself up. Pushed herself harder. I should have helped her! I should have..."

Again, grief overwhelmed words. Mac wondered if she'd ever dealt with it properly. Or if it had been buried deep down, allowed to fester, sending up those noxious gases Dan Hendry talked about. Then when Lydia's father had brought her into his confidence the resentment and the anger was all there, waiting to be unleashed.

"None of this was your fault, Hayley," Mac said gently. "You can't fix people. They have to fix themselves. You tried to help Lydia, but if she didn't want to be helped, there was nothing you or anyone could do."

"Does that apply to you?" Hayley whispered.

"For the tape please…" Isla began to say but Mac threw up a hand.

In the warm, contented afterglow they had shared that night in Kingussie, Mac had told Hayley about Iona. Told her about the panic attacks and the anger. He looked into her eyes now.

"Yes," he said simply.

"I thought maybe I could help. Until I realised the SD card was gone. I remembered where I'd put it the second I asked you to pass over my jeans. Silly, in the heat of the moment I forgot it was in there. I'm just glad you didn't find it before. I wouldn't have missed that night for anything."

Mac felt himself flush. It didn't happen often. He refused to acknowledge the questioning looks on the faces of the other two people in the room. Instead, he squeezed Hayley's hand, looking into her expressive eyes.

"Let me help you," he whispered.

Hayley nodded. Mac released her hand, though her fingers tightened around his momentarily. He returned to his seat, clearing his throat.

"Sir…" Isla began but again, he silenced her by lifting his hand.

"I think I should probably have some time with my client," the solicitor said.

Mac remembered her name suddenly. Olivia Docherty.

"No, it's OK. I don't need to," Hayley said, the tissue in her hand deteriorating into a sodden mass that she used to wipe her nose. "Ask me," she said to Mac.

"Did Daniel Webb tell you what he was planning?" Mac asked.

Inside his head he was willing Hayley to deny it. If she did he didn't want to pursue it. He didn't need to. Hayley wasn't a criminal. Maybe he was being influenced by the

205

intimacy they'd shared. Maybe his body was hoping it would be shared again. His mind however, was stepping away from her, closing off that chapter with no intention of returning.

"No," Hayley said, not looking away from Mac.

"How did you know that the picture Neill Smilley took, which was recorded onto the SD card you removed from his camera, contained images of Daniel Webb?" Mac asked.

Hayley was intelligent. Emotionally naïve, maybe. But smart. Mac couldn't help her. Couldn't prompt or lead her. She might end up in prison after all, unless she gave a convincing answer.

"Danny was angry. He was angry at the people who had led Lydia to drugs. Jake, the dealers who supplied him. The people who supplied them. We talked for a long time after the funeral. His ex-wife had been hysterical, slapping him, blaming him for always putting the service before his family. He was upset, and he was saying he was going to kill them all."

"So you did know what he was planning?" Isla put in.

"No. I just thought it was talk. I never in a million years thought he would actually go through with it. The next morning he was calm again. Like he'd come through the anger, reached the other side, you know?"

Mac felt a stab of jealousy and stamped on it.

"What happened next," he asked.

"Danny left. We'd been staying at a hotel in Blackburn. That's where Angela was from, where she'd moved back to after divorcing Danny. She wanted Lydia buried somewhere close to her parents. He left, said he was going back to Hereford."

"Hereford?" Isla asked.

"That's where his squadron was based," Hayley said.

"But within a week he'd sent me a message saying he couldn't continue in the service. That he'd resigned. I haven't heard from him since."

"Then you were assigned to the...well, let's just call it the wolf case," Mac said. "Did something make you think of Danny?"

"Just that you believed the finger belonged to Isabella North, who was linked to John Lowe. You and your team had said as much. That made me think of Danny. And when a big man in camo gear was mentioned, plus the precise nature of the shootings and the...the ferocity of the attack. Yes, I thought maybe Danny was taking his revenge. I wanted to find him. Speak to him. Maybe get him to stop. Or turn himself in. I...I don't know what I was thinking."

Mac leaned forward again, hands flat on the table. "Hayley, look at me. I understand. I do, honestly. But right now we need to find him. We can't let more people die. Have you got any way of reaching Danny?"

Hayley looked back at him searchingly then she nodded.

"Email. There's an encrypted email address. He was always paranoid. Didn't trust mobile phones or regular internet communications. Why would you once you've seen what military intelligence is capable of?"

Isla had a pen in her hand. Hayley ran a hand through her hair and put her head back, breathing out a long sigh. Her face was pale and exhausted, as though the flow of words had carried something of her spirit out with them. She recited a complex chain of characters, clearly memorised deliberately. Burned into her brain.

"Obviously if you send a message via a Police Scotland email address, he'll go to ground," Hayley said.

"We'd like you to word the message," Mac said.

"We can conceal the originating IP address through a VPN," Isla put in.

"And we're trusting that you're not tipping him off using some code you've arranged between you," Mac said.

Hayley smiled wanly. "I'm in enough trouble. I'm not involved in this. I didn't know what he was going to do. Was more afraid he would top himself, not somebody else. I'll word it so he knows it's me, but I'll say what you want."

# Chapter 23

Mac stared at a magnified close-up of the picture taken by Neill Smilley. Sandra Barnes had no pictures of her ex-husband, was seeking to expunge him from her life and memory after the death of their daughter. The Army was sympathetic about the police need for any information on one of their former soldiers, but that did not mean they were willing to co-operate. Particularly not when that soldier was a member of special forces. Mac had spoken to a Colonel who had told him in no uncertain terms that it would take a direct order from the Prime Minister to make him even admit that the SAS existed, let alone who made up its elite membership. When asked about previous regiments, Mac was referred to an officer of that regiment.

In this case it was the Lancaster Regiment. And Mac was asked for a court order and it was intimated that even a court order would be appealed. It was a maze of secrecy and bureaucracy, no-one in the British Army wanted to give information that would lead to the arrest of one of their own. Mac handed off the task to Fran Dryden who began with calls to the Home Office and Police and Crime Commissioner. It would take time. While that was being done, Daniel Webb was out there, looking to complete his mission. Complete his revenge. John Lowe would be the target.

"Maybe we should let him finish what he started," Kai said from his desk. It was the second time he'd suggested it. The first was in jest but this time Mac wasn't so sure.

Mac turned and looked over his shoulder at the sergeant.

"Sorry, guv," he muttered.

"We don't give up just because the victim happens to be a gangster. And we don't know how many innocent bystanders Webb is going to take out and dismiss as collateral damage. That's what makes him so dangerous," Mac said. "At the docks today, he killed thirty people. He may not have known that those containers contained trafficked people, but that's beside the point. Maybe the next one will be in the middle of the city, where John Lowe is having dinner at his favourite restaurant. So, what do we know?"

It was dark outside, just after six, and everyone was on overtime. Hayley had provided a detailed written statement describing her relationship with Danny Webb. The email from her had gone unanswered. Procurator Fiscal didn't want to pursue charges against her and she had been released. Mac had persuaded Dryden to sign off on personnel to follow her. Traffic units and uniform PCs in civilian clothes. In case Webb reached out to her. Or she knew more about his movements than she had let on.

"He was in Kingussie last week, killing three people," Kai said.

"He carved four lines into the tree trunk where he left

Isabella North's head," Isla volunteered, pointing to a picture of the markings with her pen.

"Four victims?" Mel thought aloud. "There were three at Kingussie so…"

"No, no, no," Mac interrupted. "Two were collateral damage. He killed them to silence them. Isabella North was one. The two dealers were two and three."

"So, one more," Kai said. "No prizes for guessing who, eh?"

"Webb could be anywhere. We don't know what timescale he's working to. Maybe he's given himself a deadline. Maybe he's biding his time, waiting for the perfect moment. Could be tomorrow or next week or next year," Mel suggested.

"We don't have to find Daniel Webb," Mac said. "Because we know where he's going to be. Wherever John Lowe is. Lowe is the fourth victim, the one responsible for the drugs getting into the hands of the street dealers. We need to find Lowe and then keep him under surveillance."

"Bait," Isla said.

Kai grinned wolfishly. "Sounds good to me, eh?"

"Shouldn't we offer him police protection?" Mel wondered aloud.

"Police protection for a gangster fighting a turf war against another gangster. Excellent use of taxpayer money, DI Barland."

Mac whirled around to see DCI Benjamin Musa in the doorway. Musa's team had been absent, not having been authorised to take overtime. Mac had timed his briefing for when the Organised Crime Taskforce was off shift. Yet here Musa stood, his long overcoat cascading around him, silhouetted by the corridor lights like Batman. He was grinning.

"This isn't a gang war, Musa," Mac said.

"Yes, that's exactly what it is and DCC Mayhew agrees with me. So, this little shindig is closed. Overtime is cancelled. You can all go home and my team will take a handover in the morning."

He strode into the office, beaming victoriously, until he stood in front of Mac. His feet were spaced apart and his hands in the pocket of his coat, held closed in front of him. It was a stereotypical alpha male pose. Combined with the extra height he had on Mac, it was a clear power play.

"A word?" Mac said, jerking his head towards his office.

"Hmmm, no. I've got to get home and put my feet up. It's been a long day doing, you know, actual police work. But good work to you and your team. This is a plot worthy of Harlan Coben right here. Really enthralling. Just a shame it's all bull. I mean, honestly, a psycho SAS soldier out to avenge his dead daughter. Please. I've seen that movie."

Mac grinned tightly, lips concealing clenched teeth.

"Still, I'd appreciate a quick word."

He turned and walked towards his office. As he did he whistled. It was a snatch of a tune, an old Rod Stewart song. The one everyone knew. As he opened the door and looked back at Musa, Mac murmured, just loud enough to be heard.

"Wake up, Maggie, I think I've got something to say to you…"

Musa's smile became fixed. He got the message. Recognised the tune and heard the name in the words. He knew what it meant. With the look of a man ready to kill, Musa followed Mac into his office. Mac slammed the door shut behind them. Musa turned to him, opening his mouth to speak. Mac hit him in the stomach with all the force he could muster. Musa grunted, folded slightly in the middle and then coughed. Mac stepped close, nose to nose.

"I know what you pay for, Benjamin. And I know who has the evidence. Maggie. You don't know where she is, right? You're paying her what she asks for and you've been looking for her but...nothing. Tell me this is another fiction, eh?"

Musa's lips peeled back from his teeth. "I. Don't. Know. What. You. Mean," he spat.

The big man tried to push past but Mac grabbed his immaculate, silk tie and yanked downward at the same time as he shove his own head forward. It caught Musa square in the mouth. This time he fell back, hands sprawling through papers on the desk he fell back. Mac moved to the door, clicked the lock shut. Musa was already on his feet when Mac turned around.

"I'm not after you. Not yet. I'll come for you, don't worry about that. One thing I can't stand is nonces," Mac hissed.

Musa growled and crossed the room in two strides, enormous hands reaching for Mac and slamming him back into the door.

"You're out of your depth. I'll give you no more warnings. I'm the Commissioner's blue-eyed boy. The DCC is in my pocket and the press love me. You, on the other hand..."

"Have caught two serial killers in the last three years," Mac reminded him. "And I'm about to catch another one. If you're in my way you're going the same way as DCI Akhtar. She thought she could play politics with people's lives. She got burned. You want to test yourself against me, Musa? Go ahead. See how many of those connections stick by you after you've been proved wrong."

Musa moved closer, putting his lips almost to Mac's ear.

"I don't care who's right or wrong. I just want to take down a gangster. Because you know what? Policemen who catch serial killers get forgotten about. Policemen who take down a criminal empire…gain the throne. You get me?"

Musa pulled his head back, eyes wide so that Mac could see the whites all the way around. The grin on Musa's face was a rictus of maniacal hate and rage. The man was dangerous and unhinged. He released Mac and stepped back, brushing at Mac's lapels, straightening his jacket.

"Glad we could have this little chat, Mac. Clear the air," Musa said in a normal voice with a neutral expression. "You're a good guy and I don't want there to be any rivalry between us. It's not good for morale or for co-operation. I think DCC Mayhew has orders for you. He's taking a more personal interest in SCU while DCS Reid is laid up. But, we can talk more tomorrow. Get some rest, yeah?"

He leaned past Mac to unlock the door, but before he opened it, he leaned in again. His voice went quieter than ever.

"If you ever threaten me with that whore again. I'll kill you and that girlfriend of yours. Her kid too, understand?"

The door was almost wrenched from its frame and Musa stalked out of the office and down the central aisle. He didn't look at Isla. Mac stepped out and smiled.

"Deputy Chief Constable Mayhew has backed the wrong horse again. He's pulling our operation. Screw him. I'm not going to order you to go against the DCC. But I'm not giving up on this. I'll risk an insubordination charge for myself. The rest of you should go home."

"With all due respect, guv," Mel said.

Then she did something Mel Barland never did. She

swore, vilely and expertly. Kai whooped and clapped. Mel blushed furiously.

"I don't have any proof to support this hunch. Its guess-work," Mac pointed out. "It's a long shot."

"You've made a career out of 'em," Kai said. "I'm in."

Mac glanced at Isla. "Oh aye, me too," she said. "I think Musa prefers to surround himself with men, anyway. Few women in his team and I've never exactly felt welcome. He won't miss me."

Mac smiled, running both hands through his hair. He tossed his suit jacket over the back of a chair and returned to the boards.

"As I was saying. We need to find John Lowe. When Webb tries to take him down, then we close the trap and hopefully take down Webb. If Mr. Lowe catches a bullet in the crossfire, I won't be grieving for him."

Kai chuckled.

"So, how do we find him? Known addresses?" Mel said.

"He has dozens," Isla said. "I've got a list for him and Hance Allen of addresses in their names and which are believed to be in their portfolios but in someone else's name. There'll be at least as many as that which we don't know about."

"The Grange, Musselburgh," Mac said, going to a map pinned up over the windows. He grabbed a marker pen and circled in red the approximate area of the Grange.

Isla opened a file on her laptop, then stood up, picking up a pen of her own. She began circling properties in a much more precise way until there were a dozen or so across Edinburgh, Fife, and the Lothians.

"That's a lot of ground to cover," Kai said.

"We'd need a hundred officers," Mel said at the same time.

215

"And it sounds like Dryden's extra bodies will be cancelled. Mayhew is cutting our strings from above. It may be just the four of us," Mac said.

Mac was staring at the map. Lowe based himself in the Edinburgh area so Webb would be here somewhere. After their confrontation earlier in the day and the explosion before that, it was likely Lowe was going to ground. Mac had already arranged for alerts at air and seaports, as well as road and railway hubs. Dryden had authorised the comms earlier in the day. The messages should have gone out. But that only worked if Lowe was trying to flee the country. If he was hunkering down, arming himself, then it wouldn't make any difference.

"I had Lowe's phone in my hand. I threw it away." Mac kicked the desk in frustration.

He'd indulged his anger. Lowe's phone might have held information that digital forensics could uncover. Something that would tell them where Lowe was hiding. A tap into his communication network. The thought of a phone made him think of another phone taken from Lowe. He froze. He'd even given Lowe a receipt for it. Mac slowly turned, mind racing. The phone would have been cleaned, wiped of anything incriminating or useful to the police. But Lowe had been using it to message Isabella's phone. And those messages were being read. Which meant that Daniel Webb had Isabella's phone.

"We've got a direct line of communication to our killer," Mac breathed.

# Chapter 24

**M**ac watched the house through a pair of night-vision binoculars. His position was amid sand dunes that formed a boundary between the Grange and the sea. Beyond him was a golf course, private and owned by John Lowe. In the centre of the golf course was the Grange itself. The windows were dark and the night-sights weren't picking up any telltale glows that would indicate a person, open or concealed. Further around the curve of the sand dunes were three other officers. They were all members of an AC squad commanded by DCI Hafsa Akhtar. DI Nari Yun monitored the Grange's single approach road while the rest of Mac's team were spread around the edges of the course. So far, there had been no sign of anyone inside.

This was just one of John Lowe's properties. They had chosen it because it was one of the more high profile, commanding its own wharf, private beach, and golf course. Everyone in Musselburgh knew the Grange was owned by someone rich. The word had gone out to the local low-life's that attempts to burgle the Grange would result in hands being cut off. It was the worst kept secret in Scotland that John Lowe was the owner. That had been the location given in the message sent from Lowe's phone to Isabella's. A message in which Mac, as Lowe, offered Daniel Webb a job. Mac hadn't thought that insults or challenges would work. Webb had planned everything thus far, meticulously. He wouldn't rush in after a message challenging him to a face off.

Instead, Mac had channeled his inner gangster. How would a man like John Lowe react to the knowledge that someone wanted to kill him, was hunting him, picking apart his operation one piece at a time? By trying to buy him. So, Mac had explained in his message that his business would benefit from a man with Webb's skills. The ruthlessness to do what needed to be done. Controlling the flow of merchandise, punishing anyone who stepped out of line. Mac bet Webb would be infuriated. To be offered a job managing the flow of drugs into the country, the same trade that had killed his daughter. The idea he could be bought, his crusade paid off, his daughter's memory cheapened, should infuriate him. It would have infuriated Mac.

"Check in," Akhtar's voice came over the radio.

"Greyhound 1. All clear," Mac spoke softly into his radio.

"Greyhound 2. All clear," Kai's voice came next.

The rest of his team checked in. Last of all was Isla, stationed at New Street, the main road from which the private access road to the Grange led.

"Greyhound 8 to Trap 1. I've got three SUVs moving eastward on New Street and all indicating left," she said, her voice humming with excitement.

Mac moved the binoculars over toward the road. The

lights over there rendered the night-sight useless. Dropping them, he thought he could see the lights of three vehicles moving slowly from right to left.

"No, no, no. Not here, you idiot," Mac breathed. "Not tonight."

Three of the four members of the AC team were firearms trained. Fran Dryden had pulled the tactical teams she had placed on standby. Mac had received a message from her saying that he was probably right but she had to follow protocol. Mayhew had pulled the overtime, cancelled the operation, and ordered all materials to be prepared for handover to Musa. Mac had needed backup and only the promise of his co-operation in taking down Kenny Reid had earned the resources of AC. At least the unit commanded by DCI Hafsa Akhtar, rescued from professional oblivion by her uncle. Mac was no longer signed off to use firearms. None of his team were. Those with firearms were strategically positioned around the most likely points of egress. The plan was to watch Daniel Webb going in, then close the trap behind him. With Webb in the Grange, he could be negotiated with safely.

Now that plan was unravelling. If John Lowe had decided to hole up at the Grange, this was potentially a blood bath.

"Trap One," Akhtar's voice sounded urgent. "Intercept before they reach the end of the approach road. Repeat intercept."

Mac cursed. That would mean unmarked cars lighting themselves up. Armed police making themselves known and surrounding Lowe's cortege. If Webb was anywhere nearby he would go to ground. He thumped his hand into the cold sand against which he lay flat. Then he saw the flash of movement below. It was a shadow flitting between shadows.

Could have been a fox or a cat. Mac brought the binoculars up just in time to see the shape of a man. He was crouching, keeping low, almost moving on his stomach through the lower reaches of the dunes. He was right below.

"Greyhound 4. I see movement at your 12 o'clock, three meters down," Mac said.

Nothing.

"Greyhound 4. Do you read?" Mac said, more urgently.

"Greyhound 8. They're turning in. Repeat they're turning in."

"Greyhound 1 to Trap 1. Do not intercept," Mac said, urgently. "Repeat, do not intercept. Webb is moving in. He is here. If we show our positions we lose him."

There was a moment's hesitation then. "Trap 1 to all units. Hold your positions. Do not intercept. Armed units prepare to move in. All unarmed units stay at the outer perimeter."

It was a smart deployment, given the likelihood of an expert marksman in their midst. But Mac had no intention of hanging back. He was trained, but his certification had lapsed. He needed to attend a training course and complete a session on a firing range to reacquire it, but had been too busy doing his job. While unarmed, he fully intended to be going in after Danny Webb. He looked down and ahead, scanning the ground with his binoculars. Another flash of movement, a small gap between two rows of shrubbery along the edge of the golf course. Mac saw it then, the dead ground that had been invisible to them when looking at the site on a map. Had remained invisible from his vantage amid the dunes. But a soldier was trained to see it, to find the smallest cover in any terrain. Webb had found it and was moving along it, concealed by a dip in the ground and the rows of plants. Mac looked ahead. It would take Webb